D0300827

ALONE

D. J. BRAZIER

ANDERSEN PRESS • LONDON

First published in 2016 by
Andersen Press Limited
20 Vauxhall Bridge Road
London SW1V 2SA
www.andersenpress.co.uk

2 4 6 8 10 9 7 5 3 1

British Library Cataloguing in Publication Data available.

ISBN 978 1 78344 403 8

Printed and bound in Great Britain by
CPI Group (UK) Ltd, Croydon CR0 4YY

For Mum

PART ONE

ONE

I'm being boiled alive.

Waves of searing heat roll over me. I turn my head and heave, spewing up hot water thick with aviation fuel. It burns my already scorched throat.

Something explodes on the other side of the plane and I try to duck but the life jacket keeps me vertical and I can't dip my head below the surface. Another explosion, the biggest yet, ignites the fuel slick and a ring of flame encircles me, so close it blinds me. I dig my fingers into the life jacket and scream, 'Dad!' again and again. There's no reply, just the roar of the flames. A finger of fire jabs my cheek, blistering the skin. I can hardly breathe in the thick smoke and I can smell my hair singeing. I have to get away. But I don't know how. My head is pounding and I can't think clearly. There's too much noise, too much smoke, heat and confusion.

I can't swim through the flames. I'll have to try to dive beneath them. And I have to do it now.

I take the life jacket off. Without its buoyancy to support me, the weight of my heavy jeans and trainers pulls me under and I swallow more water. I claw my way back to the surface, throw the life jacket through the flames, take a deep breath and dive. I swim as hard as I can, kicking my legs, desperately trying to clear the fire above. The water is pitch black and I have no idea how wide the flaming wall is but I keep going as long as I can, heading away from the heat and noise until it feels like my lungs are about to burst and I can stay under no longer. I break the surface, coughing and retching. The flames and smoke are behind me. Ahead is just blackness and bullets of silver rain. Something soft bumps against me – the life jacket, smouldering and half-submerged. I grab it and pull it on, and as I do so a piece of material floats free. In the flickering light from the flames something familiar about the fabric's colouring and pattern catches my eye and I scoop it up before it drifts out of reach. Holding it close to my stinging eyes, I squint at the checked material and immediately recognise it. It's the ripped chest pocket of a shirt. Dad's shirt.

Another explosion behind me. Something slams into the back of my head, and everything goes black.

TWO

I wake slowly, drifting back to consciousness. My head is throbbing and it takes me a moment or two to realise I'm lying on a beach with my blistered cheek pressed into hot sand and my arm twisted painfully beneath me. At first I have no idea where I am or how I got here, but then memories of the plane crash come flooding back – the storm, the screaming engines. The fire. Dad's shirt pocket.

Dad!

The sun's glare blinds me as I rise unsteadily to my feet and yell, 'Dad! Dad!' and, 'Help! Please. Somebody help me,' over and over again until it's too painful to yell any more.

I hesitantly probe a painful lump on the back of my head, matted with dried blood and hair, then shield my eyes and look around me. The sandspit I've washed up on slopes down to a fast-flowing river, wide and brown. Behind me the jungle is dark and dense, and unbelievably loud with the cries of birds and other creatures.

The inside of my mouth feels like I've been chewing sandpaper and I have a raging thirst. I take off my life jacket and walk to the river's edge, swerving to avoid stepping on an eyeless fish crawling with ants and flies. The water is lukewarm and murky in my cupped hands, but after a moment's hesitation I take a sip. It tastes stale, and flat, like a fizzy drink left in the sun. But at least it's wet, and partially soothes my burnt throat, so I sink my face in the river and gulp until I can stand the taste no longer.

The last decent drink I had was a Coke at the airport, guzzled down while Dad called Mum to tell her we were on our way home. I can see him clearly in my mind, phone in one hand and a packet of crisps in the other, chuckling as he teased Mum about the state of the Single Prop plane we were about to board. The plane to take us on the last leg of our journey back to the main airport. Then in two days we'd be home.

My shoulders slump. I turn and walk to the shade of a tree and sit down with my back against the trunk. Hugging my knees to my chest, I squeeze my eyes shut and try to work out how in hell I got here.

'The trip of a lifetime.' That's what it was supposed to be. Paid for with the money Gran left me. Money she made me promise to spend on a great adventure, and not just 'fritter away'. She'd been saving for years in preparation for the day when she and Grandpa could go on their own dream trip.

But life kept getting in the way, she said. Then she got ill. Then she died. But before she got too sick she put all the money in a bank account and made me promise I'd make the trip for her, and see the world, especially the jungle, and do it now, before it was too late. With one condition – Dad had to come.

Dad didn't want to. 'Things aren't good at work, Sam,' he said. 'I can't afford to take the time off.' His usual excuse. But I pleaded and pestered, wearing him down, and I even played the 'But we never do anything together' card, and I could tell he was wavering. Then Mum helped, after I'd worn her down too. 'It's what your mum wanted,' she told him, and she said it would be good for Dad and me to spend some father and son time together, and who knows, he might even enjoy it. Dad laughed and said Mum just wanted some peace and quiet on her own, but I could tell he knew Mum was right.

And this trip with Dad has been brilliant. Even better than I hoped. We've seen and done some amazing things and I've never seen him laugh so much as he has in the past three weeks. At times I've hardly recognised him. Having him all to myself has been incredible. There's been time to talk. About anything and everything. About things we've never spoken about before. About how I can't talk to girls. How badly I sometimes want a brother or sister, or better still a dog, and how I hate being shorter than all my friends. And even though I'm not sure he really understood, he listened, properly for once, and that's enough. Then he told me things too; about his life before I came along. About how much he hates his job sometimes, and that's why he's so hard on me about doing my homework and not 'wasting my life' on Minecraft. He talked about what happened when he first met Mum – how shy he was, and how long it took him to find the courage to say hello to her, then to ask her out. Then he said, 'Lucky for you I didn't give up, eh?' and grossed me out.

A loud screech comes from the undergrowth, and I jump to my feet and spin round but I can't see anything in the dense foliage.

Still thinking about Dad, I walk to the top end of the sandspit, past a crooked tree overhanging the water, and peer upriver for any sign of the plane. But I can only see a little way upstream, to a bend in the river, and with a sinking feeling I realise I have no idea how far I drifted from the plane after I blacked out.

Sweat drips from my brow and I can feel my arms burning in the hot sun, but thankfully there's a stream here, winding out from the jungle, and the water tastes clean and far fresher than the river. So I drink until my stomach's full and sit in the shade, rocking gently back and forth, trying to figure out what to do.

I could go looking for the plane.

No. Stupid idea!

It could be miles away, and before the trip began Dad made me promise that if we ever got separated I was to stay where I was, and he would find me, however long it took. And he will. I know he will. Dad doesn't make many promises, but when he does, he keeps them. I just have to wait.

Something tickles my neck. A small brown ant. It scurries down my arm and halts at my elbow, feelers waving. I try to gently brush it off without killing it, but as soon as my hand touches the ant it bites me. Tiny needle jaws pinch my skin, and I yelp, more in surprise than pain, trying to flick it away. But it clings on, and is quickly joined by dozens more. I jump to my feet and thrash my arm up and down, trying to shake them off, but they just tighten their grip and hang on. Glancing at the tree I've been leaning against I see a long column of ants streaming down the trunk and out onto the sand towards the dead fish. I've put myself between the ants and their meal and they're not happy. More swarm inside my T-shirt and nip my chest and I tear it off and run down to the river, wading in and dunking my head under the water.

I sit in the shallows for ten minutes or so, reluctant to leave the cool water, until I feel the skin on the back of my neck burning and begin to think about what sort of creatures could be lurking in the dark waters. Something calls close by, a sort of barking sound, followed by a big splash. I leave the river.

Walking the other way along the sandspit, I slump down in the shade beneath the tallest tree I can find — a giant which towers over the others.

Hours pass. I call for Dad and for help repeatedly, but with no reply. The sun climbs higher, the air gets hotter and more humid, and each trip to the stream for a drink leaves me drenched in sweat. I sit and scratch at the ant bites itching on my arm, or tug at my tangled hair, and hope Dad is close by.

By mid-afternoon I'm bored and starving and I can't sit still any longer. I have to do something. Search for food, bathe my blistered arms, or make a *HELP* sign out of driftwood perhaps. No. The sun is still too hot.

Then I jump to my feet. I've had a brilliant idea! I'll climb a tree and find out where I am. With any luck I'll be able to spot the plane close by, or a village, or a boat. Climbing I can do, it's one of the few things I'm good at. Excited by the thought of rescue, I grab a thick vine entwined around the giant tree's trunk and make a start, not bothering with the long, hot walk for a drink first.

The tree isn't hard to climb. Thick vines provide plenty of hand- and footholds and I make good progress to begin with. But after half an hour or so, the vines end and branches from neighbouring trees intertwine to create a dense barrier. I have to force my way between them, sometimes leaning right out into space, telling myself not to look down, and hoping the next branch or vine I reach for doesn't snap in my hand.

After another hour of twisting and wriggling, I'm exhausted, dripping in sweat and unbearably thirsty. The climb is far harder and more demanding than I expected and I reckon it will take me another two or three hours at least to fight my way through the rest of the canopy stretching high above. I slump back against the trunk and tear twigs from my hair. My brilliant idea has backfired. I'm worn out, dizzy and higher than I've ever been before. It would be beyond stupid to try climbing any further. Unless I head back now I may not make it down before nightfall.

I pluck a leaf from my clammy brow and as I do so I notice a mass of flowers directly above me, snow white and dotted with yellow spots like miniature suns, and hearts of stunning scarlet. They are the most beautiful flowers I have ever seen and I know what they are. Orchids. Mum's favourite! Dad always buys them for her birthday and she has them all over the house. But these orchids are much bigger than any I've seen before, and far more impressive than anything stuck in a pot. And best of all, where the leaves meet at the stems' base they form a cup, full of rainwater.

I tilt the plant towards me and greedily slurp the water, after picking out a couple of drowning bugs first. I don't know what else is in the water but as I gulp it down it's like drinking one of those energy drinks my mates sometimes share but Mum won't buy me. Well, whatever is in the water works, and the energy boost is more than enough to convince me to keep climbing. I reach for the branch the orchids are growing on, and pull myself up.

Finally my head breaks through the canopy and my eyes snap shut. After so long in semi-darkness the dazzling brightness of the sun bores into my skull. Eager as I am to take a look around, I have to wait until the dancing dots fade from my eyelids before I dare open my eyes.

My heart drops. The jungle stretches as far as I can see in every direction, immense and never-ending. Nothing breaks the carpet of green. Nothing but the river below me, which I can now see is no more than a skinny worm in comparison to the giant brown snake it flows into – the Amazon. There's no sign of the plane. Or a village or town. No buildings. No smoke curling up from the trees. No boats. Nothing.

I cup my hands and yell, 'Dad!' and, 'Help!' a dozen times but all I get in reply is screeching birds taking flight, and monkeys howling at the sound of my shrill voice. I am alone.

THREE

The night seems endless. Sleep is impossible. The nightmares are bad enough, reliving the crash and waking screaming and shivering with fear. But the dreams are worse. At least, waking from them is. The slow, painful realisation that I'm not in bed at home and it isn't the television I can hear.

I try lying down but the ground is too hard and uneven, and insects swarm all over me. So I sit upright, arms clasped around my knees, trembling and tense, dreading the next rustle in the undergrowth, or harsh scream signalling the death of another poor creature.

The jungle is black, loud and menacing, and I have no way of telling what may be crouched within the foliage, watching me, impatiently waiting for me to fall asleep, drooling with hunger at the scent of my sweaty body. But a few terrifying possibilities come to mind. My teacher says I'm lucky to have such a vivid imagination, but I don't feel lucky now.

I rub my cold legs, and try to convince myself there are no monsters lurking in the darkness. But I can't. The dark is too thick and sinister, too threatening. This isn't the soft dark that fills my room when I'm warm and comfortable beneath my duvet. This dark is solid. Impenetrable.

The night drags on. Hordes of insects crawl all over me. In the black jungle creatures howl and fight and kill and feed. I am more tired than I have ever been, but I'm too cold and frightened to sleep and I can't rest knowing there is no other human being for miles around. Perhaps even hundreds or thousands of miles in every direction.

I have never felt so lonely.

Some sort of beetle crash-lands in my hair and I scream. I jump to my feet and rake it out, vigorously rubbing my numb arms and legs. This is torture. I so badly want to be in my bed right now, with my duvet and soft pillow and the muffled sounds of the television downstairs. I want something to eat. I want Dad to find me. I want Mum. But more than anything, I want it to be light again.

***

Finally dawn comes. Black fades to grey and the horizon pales to the colour of weak orange squash. Birds sing in the trees and fog blankets the river. After a short while the fog clears and the sun shines through, bringing warmth and light.

And mosquitoes.

At first they appear in ones and twos, jigging in front of my eyes, as if sizing me up. I clap my hands and splat two in quick succession. But loads more arrive and land on my exposed skin. I slap angrily at the ones feasting on my sunburnt neck but there are too many of them and the itching becomes unbearable. So I run. I run along the sandspit, flailing my arms above my head and the mosquitoes follow me, hovering, taunting me with their whiny laughter and dropping back down to bite me as soon as I lower my arms.

But the sun is already too hot and I am too tired to run in the soft sand for long. I wade into the river and sit down instead, submerged up to my eyes with my T-shirt draped over my head while I try to figure out what to do.

I could head into the jungle; at least it will be cooler in there and perhaps I'll find food and shelter and the mosquitoes won't follow me. But then again I could get lost pretty quickly and after last night, the idea of spending a night deep in the dark jungle is too horrible to bear. And anyway, surely by now the non-arrival of our plane has been reported and search parties dispatched. If so they will be tracing the plane's flight path, looking for wreckage and if I leave the river and head into the jungle, there's no way a helicopter or plane could spot me. No. My best chance of being seen is if I stay by the river.

I could head upriver to look for the plane. With any luck most of it could still be intact and if I can reach the crash site then I stand a far better chance of being found. And finding Dad.

Plus my phone is on the plane, in my rucksack, along with chewing gum and chocolate and even if I can't get a signal, the plane's radio might still be working and there will be other stuff I can use, like signal flares and perhaps even matches to light a fire. I could so do with a fire. As well as the light and warmth it would provide, the smoke would act as a signal to the search teams and keep the mosquitoes at bay. But then I stare at the thick, dark jungle pressed up against the edge of the river and decide against it. It's too risky. Chances are the plane burnt up and sank. And even if it's still partially intact, I have no idea how long it might take to find it. It could be days away and the truth is I'm too frightened, not just of what might be lurking in the jungle, but of what I might discover in the wreckage if I do find it.

No. I have fresh water here, and shade. Dad and the rescue party will know how to find me. The only sensible thing for me to do is to stay where I am. Like Dad told me to.

By mid-morning the heat and humidity have risen drastically and my clothes are soaked through. But at least the mosquitoes have gone. My gurgling stomach keeps reminding me how hungry I am, and I really should search for food but it's just too hot, and the only way I can escape the heat is to stay in the shade. Or wade into the river. Both options suck. The shade is full of scurrying, biting insects hiding from the sun, and although the river is cool I'm sure I felt something brush against my leg the last time I entered the water. So for now I have reluctantly decided that the bugs are the least dangerous option and I'm sticking to dry land. I yawn, and stretch my arms high above my head. I'm exhausted after yesterday's climb and a sleepless night, and despite the heat and my hunger I soon doze off.

When I wake, the air is noticeably cooler and the sun much lower in the sky. I hurry to the stream to drink and bathe my arms, and as I reach the end of the sandspit a black bird skims across the river, hooking a fat fish with its bill, and I glower at it. It's been two days since I last ate – a bar of Galaxy on the plane. I close my eyes and lick my cracked lips and then for the hundredth time I check my pockets for a stray piece of chewing gum or even a peanut, but all I find is fluff and tiny balls of tissue.

I kick out at the picked-clean white bones which is all the ants have left of the dead fish, and decide it's now cool enough for me to explore the rest of the sandspit.

Bits of wood, stones and a few strange-looking snail shells litter the shore but nothing that looks remotely edible. But then right at the far end I find a leafy branch snagged between two rocks and when I flick it over I uncover two roundish green fruit that look like some sort of fig. They're weird and alien-looking. But there is nothing else so reluctantly I return to my tree.

After another hour or so spent chewing my nails and trying to ignore the pangs of hunger cramping my stomach I head back to the figs. I still don't like the look of them but it'll soon be dark and I'm too hungry to care. I twist the fruit off the branch, tear the skin away and hesitantly nibble the green insides. The flesh is hard, and bitter, and I spit it out and hurl the fig into the river. It lands with a loud plop only a few metres from the far bank. I rip the second one from the branch and I'm about to see if I can clear the river with this one when something appears in the water close to where the fig landed. A brown whiskered face, like a seal's. No, more like a cat's. Staring at me. Then I hear a whistling sound, coming from upriver. I turn and peer in the direction of the sound and can just about see some sort of creature lying on a rock further up the opposite side of the river. At first I presume it's a caiman but in the dim evening light it's impossible to tell. Curious, I take a step towards it. But as soon as I do, the creature slips into the water and when I look back, the brown whiskered face has vanished too.

I lower my arm and only then do I notice that this fruit is different from the first. It's redder and softer, like a tomato. I turn it over and peel back the skin, which comes away more easily than the first one and this time the flesh is amber-coloured, a bit like a peach. I raise the fruit to my lips and take a bite. A glutinous substance oozes out, bulging with tiny black seeds. The pulp doesn't really taste of anything and the seeds have a sharp peppery taste, but I'm too hungry to care and I swallow them anyway. I scrape every last scrap of flesh from the skin and suck my fingers dry. One fig barely makes a dent in my hunger and I scan around for more.

No more than two or three minutes later the first stomach cramps hit. I double up in agony and fall to my knees, clutching my stomach, which starts to make horrible noises. I just about manage to step out of my jeans and kick my pants off before my bowels empty with a whoosh, and yellowy brown liquid oozes down my legs and pools on the sand. The stench is disgusting, to me at least. But the flies seem to love it as they quickly zero in on the mess and crawl across my bum. I can't bear their prickly feet on my skin and I pull my pants and jeans back on and writhe on the sand.

I don't know how long I lie there, stinking and sobbing, shivering and soaked with sweat. But I do know I'm dying. I'm sure of it. What a pathetic, stupid way to die! But at least the pain will be over soon.

To my surprise I'm still alive when dusk falls, and the cramps have eased enough for me to be able to crawl back to my tree. I should be grateful I'm still alive. But I'm not. I'm feeling too sorry for myself, and too miserable at the thought of spending another sleepless night alone, scared, cold and hungry. And covered in my own crap.

FOUR

My stomach has never been so empty. Or my mind so obsessed with food.

I'm starving. I used to say that all the time, without thinking, but now for the first time in my life I know what the word means. What total fear and desperation feels like. The stomach cramps. The headaches. The twisting, burning feeling in my guts. The shivering and clammy skin. And I will do anything to stop this pain.

I lift my shoe. My lips curl in disgust as I stare down at a blurry white creature writhing on the ground. It's a fat grub the size of my thumb.

A large part of me cannot believe I am even considering doing what I am about to. But the stomach cramps are unbearable and I have seen enough Bear Grylls episodes to know that this revolting package is full of protein and might just save my life. And

I have to do it now, while it's getting dark and I'm not confronted with its bulging podgy body and bulbous glossy brown head.

I pick the grub up and it thrashes between my fingers, struggling to escape. I breathe deeply a few times, trying to settle the nausea rising in my throat. Decision time. Do I bite the head off or do I swallow it whole? The thought of gulping it down whole is the least repulsive option, but then again what if it survives in my stomach and crawls around my guts, gorging on my organs? My mind is made up. I raise the grub to my lips, insert its hideous head in my mouth, close my eyes, and bite.

As soon as the tips of my teeth touch its skin the grub tenses and whips its body to and fro. I tighten my grip and bite down hard. The skin bursts and a snot-like substance fills my mouth, a revolting gob of warm goo, like a heavy cold, but worse, and tasting more disgusting than all the things I detest rolled into one – celery, liver and mushy peas. My body instantly rejects it and I throw up, just like I did when I tried to eat a snail I found beneath a rock in the river. It's no good. I can't help it. Starving or not, I don't have the stomach for this.

I wipe my mouth on my wet T-shirt, and for the hundredth time since sunset, I hug my knees and close my eyes and try to sleep. Only when I sleep do I forget how hungry I am. How scared. How alone. But sleep won't come. I'm too hungry. Too cold and wet and itchy. Too miserable. Too tired.

I used to long for more 'alone' time. To wish Mum would just leave me by myself and not pester me every five minutes. But now I realise I've never really been alone before. Not like this. Even in my room, with the door locked and no one else in the house, there was always my phone or the computer. Always a way to contact someone when I wanted to. Well, that's all gone now and for the first time in my life I am truly on my own, completely alone.

At last dawn comes, its arrival announced by the usual annoying racket of birds and monkeys, and a multitude of other animals I have no desire to even attempt to identify. I sit up and cough, and try not to retch as I pick bits of fig and grub skin from between my furry teeth. I need a drink and to wash my mouth out, but I'll wait until I'm warmer, and really thirsty. It's the only way I can bear the mosquitoes.

Parrots stream from the trees, hundreds of them, flashing blue and red and squawking happily as they head out to fill their bellies, and I hate them. I hate them for their freedom to fly high above the trees and go wherever they want to. I hate them for having a chance to escape.

Picking up a stick, I turn my back on the parrots and decide to make a list of the things I miss most. The first one is easy. But then, with the stick's tip resting on the ground, I pause, and decide to write my second choice first.

FOOD. Chocolate. Crisps. Chips. Cheese, tuna, ham, and sausage sandwiches. Bacon and eggs. Fish fingers. Baked beans. Ice cream. And much to my surprise – peas and carrots.

DRINKS. A chilled pint of fizzing Coke. Fresh milk straight from the fridge. A strawberry and banana smoothie. Hot chocolate at night-time.

MY BED!

DRY comes next: dry clothes – a clean and dry, sweet-smelling T-shirt that doesn't feel like a crusty dishcloth. Warm and dry cotton socks that don't itch and stink. Pants. Soft, clean ones that don't chafe my sore bum like sandpaper; which leads me straight to *TOILET PAPER* and *OINTMENT.*

A TOOTHBRUSH and paste, so my mouth doesn't taste like it's full of fur and grit.

VOICES. Boy, how I miss conversation! I had no idea how noisy my life was before. How many times the sounds of voices filled my ears. The TV. The radio.

Skype. Friends blabbering on the phone. Then before I realise it I have scratched the first letter of the word I intended to write first but couldn't bring myself to. I've written an 'M'.

The stick falls from my hand. I can write no more. Like all my ideas, this was a stupid one. I grab my stick and destroy my childish scribbling, digging and gouging until no letters remain.

I'm really annoyed now, and angry enough to try to burst the boil on my nose again, the one which appeared yesterday evening, and has sprouted to the size of a Malteser. I squeeze the base of the boil as hard as I can between my forefingers and this time the skin splits and to my horror a ribbon of wriggling white worms spews from the wound and dribbles onto my lips. Pus and blood would have been bad enough but this is beyond disgusting! I scream, and spit, and raise my hand to wipe the worms away, but as I do so I see the dull red blur of a mosquito perched on the peak of one knuckle, guzzling my blood, and I snap.

Howling and jumping to my feet I slap my knuckle as hard as I can, over and over, splattering the mosquito, and I keep slapping long after its mangled body is spread across the back of my hand and my sore knuckles are stained red from the pummelling.

I am consumed with hatred for the jungle. And everything in it, and everything about it. I hate the unrelenting heat and humidity. I detest the cold and sleepless nights. The rain. I loathe the blood-stealing mosquitoes, ticks and leeches. The spiders, flies and worms. I hate every single thing that scurries or scuttles or slithers or crawls in this hell.

It wasn't supposed to be like this. Not according to Gran and the stack of *National Geographic*s she left me and which I read from cover to cover, over and over again. Or the documentaries I devoured, and the countless hours I spent online. The jungle was meant to be exotic and beautiful, thrilling and wonderful. Well, the magazines lied. So did the TV and the Internet. And so did Gran.

There's nothing exotic about starvation, stomach cramps and sleepless, terrifying nights. Nothing beautiful about skin-blistering sunburn, blinding headaches and puking up grubs. Nothing thrilling about worms spewing from your face, mosquitoes, boils and blisters. Nothing wonderful about digging ticks out of your pubic hair and trying to live with chronic diarrhoea and a cracked and bleeding arse.

No. It was a lie. The truth is the jungle is a bitch. The jungle is a bully.

Black flies land on the raw skin of my weeping nose. With a layer of skin removed it feels like their tiny clawed feet are tugging directly on my nerve endings. They're too infuriating to ignore and every few seconds I scream and brush them from my nose. I can't take this! Time for a drink, and to wash off the flies and worms.

Grey fog blankets the river. The stream water is cool and refreshing and I drink as much as I can, hoping a full stomach will alleviate some of my hunger. But the sudden intake of so much fluid stirs something in my bowels and before I can clean my face properly I'm seized with cramps and an urgency to poo. I hitch up my jeans and shuffle towards the clump of bushes I've been using as a toilet. But as I approach the bushes the breeze changes direction and gusts into my face; I get a whiff of the area. It stinks. Absolutely reeks. Reluctantly I head around the bend.

Hurriedly stepping out of my jeans and crusty pants, I squat, and a stream of pale green liquid streams onto the sand. My guts still feel uncomfortably clogged so I wait for a few minutes more but nothing else comes.

Now pestered by flies and impatient to clean myself, I crawl towards the river. As I reach the water's edge the fog lifts and I can see the seal-like creature I caught a glimpse of on the first day, lying on a rock. And then I realise that what at first sight looked like one animal is in fact two. And I know what they are. They're not seals. Or cats. Or caimans. They're otters! A mother and her pup. I gasp and drop to the sand.

As my chest hits the wet sand the mother otter bolts upright, and stands erect on her hind feet, front paws bent, nose held high and whiskers twitching, sniffing the air. She's so big! Taller than me! Far bigger than the otters in the zoo. Shimmering orange butterflies swarm around her head but she ignores them and continues to taste the breeze and stare in my direction, listening intently. I hold my breath and stay as still as I can, frightened she will see me and disappear.

Fortunately the wind is blowing across the river from the otters to me, carrying my scent away from her, and after a short while she relaxes and drops back down onto the rock and licks the face of her pup, who hasn't stopped chirping and tugging her fur, demanding attention. Then she barks and slides into the water. The pup lunges at her tail as she goes, then leaps high in the air trying to catch a butterfly.

Staying still and silent I stare across the river, watching the pup play until his mother returns and bounds onto the rock with a round silver and red fish flapping in her jaws – a piranha! The pup makes a grab for the fish and his mother lets him take it before sliding back into the water and quickly returning with breakfast for herself, another plump piranha.

Still lying on the wet sand, I enviously watch the otters eat, crunching through fish scales and bones with ease and gulping down strips of flesh, and for a second or two I think about swimming across the river and nicking one from them, until the mother yawns, jaws stretched wide, displaying a wicked set of curved, bone-crunching canines. Teeth... Piranhas... I stay where I am.

It takes the mother no time at all to consume her fish, and when the pup has finished his as well they both enter the river to wash. And play. Together.

Owww! Sand flies have discovered my bare flesh and are starting to bite, but I resist the urge to swat them or risk creeping into the river. I'm too scared of frightening the otters away.

Playtime over, the mother returns to the rock and stretches out to dry herself in the sun, but her pup won't let her. He clambers all over her, tugging her whiskers and nipping her webbed feet until she's had enough and lifts a paw to clout him. He squeaks with delight and dives into the water, bobbing close to the rock, impatiently watching Mum until she closes her eyes and he can creep slowly up onto the rock and pounce on her once more. This time she grabs him in a bear hug and they roll off the rock and into the water together. Mum lets the pup go and climbs back onto the rock and starts to clean herself, but instead of following her, the pup turns. He starts to swim away from the rock and his mother, directly towards me, and I press myself flat against the sand, worried he's seen me. But just as he enters the strong midstream current his mother calls him back with a burst of loud barks and whistles. The pup stops and hesitates, peering in my direction. His mum barks again, more harshly this time, and he turns and slowly swims back to her, squeaking softly. I can tell he knows he's in trouble for straying too far, and when he reaches Mum she jumps on him and gives him a nip and a cuff for being disobedient, and the pup squeals and squirms beneath her.

His punishment isn't exactly severe though, and within seconds of telling him off Mum's licking the pup's face, nibbling his head and grooming his velvety coat. The pup sighs and snuggles against his mother and she wraps her front paws around him and nuzzles his head, and suddenly I'm swamped by a sudden wave of envy. I want my mum to hug me, and kiss my head, and ruffle my hair. I want to feel like the pup: loved and safe.

The breeze changes direction and the mother otter catches my scent. In an instant she seizes her pup by his neck and leaps from the rock. They both vanish beneath the surface.

I stay still for a few moments longer, scanning the river, hoping the otters will reappear. But I can bear the flies and mosquitoes no longer, and I jump to my feet and slap my arse and the back of my legs repeatedly.

After quickly washing myself in the river, I take a long look at the otters' rock, now covered in butterflies, before collecting my pants and jeans and heading back to my tree, lost in thought, not even bothering to scan the cloudless sky for planes on the way.

For the rest of the day, and until long after sunset, I sit in the sweltering heat and humidity and dab at a weeping boil that won't dry, scratch soft scabs from insect bites that won't heal, and hurry to the stream more frequently than before, to gulp water that the sun then steals from my sweaty, sunburnt skin. And all the while I gaze across the river at a bare and silent rock before ambling back to my tree to wait for a rescue that does not come.

I replay every moment of the encounter with the otters over and over. Every detail – the first sight through the fog. The piranhas. The butterflies. The play and grooming. The chattering. The cuddles.

I want to be held like that. I want one of Mum's full-on hugs, when I bury my face in her jumper and she squeezes me just hard enough that I can feel her heart pulsing through my cheek as she strokes my back and tells me she's got me now and everything is going to be all right. I want someone to talk to. I don't want to be alone any more.

For the first time since the crash I know exactly what I have to do. I have to go home. I have to find the plane.

FIVE

As soon as it's light enough to see, I call for Dad, but without as much enthusiasm as before. It's too depressing hearing nothing in reply. Too painful a reminder of how alone I am. And something's been bothering me about my memories of Dad and the crash. No matter how hard I try, I can't remember anything that happened between when I put my headphones on, shortly after take-off, and finding myself treading water, surrounded by flames. I don't know what happened to Dad. For all I know he could have injured himself and got trapped in the wreckage. Or perhaps he was knocked unconscious and he's wandering around in a daze, and that's why he hasn't found me yet.

The more I think about it, the more I realise I was wrong, I should have tried to find the plane right away, not just sit on my arse feeling sorry for myself like I have done for the past few days. I so want to believe a rescue team will find me today but what if it doesn't? What if no one finds me until the day after tomorrow, or the next day, or the day after that? What if no one ever comes. I have no way of knowing when or even if a search team will check this area but I do know that if I want to stay alive long enough to be found then I'm going to have to help myself. I'm going to have to face reality. I have no food. No matches. No knife. No medicine. Everything that could be of use to me is on the plane.

The thought of having to fight my way through the jungle makes my stomach churn but the thought of spending another cold and hungry night alone is worse.

If I can find Dad I'll be fine. I know I will. And with any luck I may not have to enter the jungle at all. I know the plane ended up in the river. I have my life jacket and hopefully the crash site won't be too far upstream. If I keep to the river then I'll have plenty of water to drink and if a helicopter or plane does come today then they will still be able to see me.

Before I set out I make a big *HELP* sign on the beach out of stones and driftwood. If anyone flies overhead then at least they'll know someone's still alive. I pull the life jacket over my head and tie the long strings. It's hot and uncomfortable but I won't enter the river without it.

Walking along the riverbank is much harder than I expected. The bright sunlight reflecting off the sand blinds me, and grit fills my trainers, grating my feet, and I have to stop every few paces to empty them. Sweat stings my eyes and my legs feel unbearably heavy and hot. I can't describe this as a walk, or even a hike. This is more like a punishment.

No more than an hour's trek from the sandspit, the riverbank disappears beneath a mesh of thick tree roots and I have no choice but to wade out into the river to get past them. The strong current pulls at my legs and I grip the roots hard to keep my balance. I clear one long clump but a little further on another tangle of roots blocks my way and this one extends even further into the river than the last. I clamber up onto a thick root and peer upriver but there's still no sign of the plane.

My wet jeans cling to my legs, chafing my crotch, and I'm tempted to turn back. But I think of Dad again. What if he's lying injured and slowly bleeding to death? I look back at the way I've come then splash water on my face, leave the river, and head into the jungle.

SIX

The harsh sunlight softens the moment I enter the jungle, and I have to lean against a tree for balance while my eyes adjust. The air is heavy and still and it's much quieter as well. The sounds of screeching birds and buzzing insects are muffled in here and my feet make no sound on a spongy carpet of moss and leaf litter. My feet are sore and my socks are full of grit and I consider going barefoot. But then I think about what could be concealed in the decomposing mush and decide against it.

I struggle on for an hour or so, trying to keep the river in sight, but the vegetation is thickest along the riverbank and I'm forced to head deeper into the jungle.

It's brutally hard. Ants fall from branches as I brush past, and burrow into my hair, biting my scalp and ears, and every few paces a plant whips, claws or scratches me. Or some sort of insect stings me.

After another backbreaking hour or two, a belt of thorn bushes blocks my way. They're much taller than I am and I can see no way through. I pick up a stick and slash at the bushes. A bird the size of a pigeon bursts from the thicket and hovers above my head, squawking and flapping its wings. As I cower and raise my stick above my head for protection the bird lands in a tree a short distance away. I stand and notice my thrashing stick has created a hole in the thicket. I can see a nest woven in the bush. Reaching my arm through the thorny branches I probe the nest with my fingers. Yes! Eggs. Four of them. Warm and smooth. I carefully close my hand around one and withdraw it.

The egg sits in my cupped hand, cream-coloured with blue and yellow spots. The mother starts screeching again and beating her wings; I hesitate, but saliva fills my mouth and I hurriedly crack the egg on a branch. In my haste I hit the branch too hard and the egg disintegrates, the gooey contents coating the branch and dribbling to the ground. I swear, take a deep breath and tell myself to calm down and be more careful before reaching back into the nest to take another one. I place this one in my mouth whole and slowly crack the shell with my teeth. The sticky contents and mashed-up shell trickle down my throat, and I think back to when I would refuse to touch a boiled egg if the yolk wasn't perfectly cooked or the white bit was even a little bit runny. But I've never been this hungry before.

The third egg I savour a little more, swirling the thick liquid around my cheeks before swallowing it. I reach into the nest to grab the last egg, and pause. The mother bird is still frantically clucking away and hungry as I am it doesn't seem right to take all her eggs. I withdraw my hand and walk away. A few metres further along the thorn barrier I find a spot where the bushes are less dense and using my stick I slash my way through, ignoring the thorns tearing my skin. I break through to a clearing. And stop.

A vast swamp stretches ahead of me, wide and dark and still, and extending as far as I can see.

SEVEN

In the hazy light beneath the canopy the swamp seems to have two surfaces. A still dark green one, and a grey one hovering just above, and with a shiver I realise what it is – mosquitoes! Millions of them. This must be where they come to escape the midday heat. The thought of wading through the centre of that stabbing swarm makes me want to throw. But I have no choice. I've come too far to turn back now, and even if I did there's no way I could make it back to the sandspit before nightfall. And for all I know the plane could be on the other side of the swamp, with Dad trapped inside. I have to keep going, and I have to cross the swamp as quickly as I can.

I take the life jacket and my T-shirt off and drape it over my head for protection. Then I put the life jacket back on, and after tucking my T-shirt into the jacket collar and adjusting it so I have a slit to look through, I step into the swamp, and sink up to my chest in cold, cloying liquid. The mosquitoes descend immediately, and swarm around the gap in my T-shirt, determined to find a way in.

Slime coats my arms and chest and my shuffling feet disturb pockets of trapped gas which rise and burst on the surface, releasing a stench so foul and putrid I gag. My eyes water. But to my horror it seems that either the scent of the gas or my salty tears excite the mosquitoes and the deeper I wade into the swamp the angrier they become. And these mosquitoes appear to be bigger and even more aggressive than the ones on the sandspit. I soon realise that this disgusting swamp is their patch, their home, and I have invaded it. Tens of thousands swarm around my head and shoulders, a whining, maddening storm of dentist's drills, and I dare not pause to try to defend myself.

So many crowd around the gap in my T-shirt that I can barely see where I'm going and I can only hope I'm heading the right way. My legs grow heavier with each demanding lunge and it takes every ounce of strength I have to keep going.

The sludge deepens until it's sucking at my armpits and only my life jacket prevents me from going under.

I'm shivering, partly from the cold and partly from the fear that the swamp may get even deeper. The thought of drowning in this putrid swill terrifies me and I'm constantly fighting the urge to turn back. Wading through the swamp is far more exhausting than I could have imagined, and I know that if I don't get out soon then I will never leave this place. I will simply run out of energy and sink beneath the surface, or give in to the mosquitoes and the gas.

Bushes rustle to my right and in my mind I see a snake, huge and hungry, slithering towards me.

I take another painful step and the swamp floor falls away beneath me.

I doggy paddle furiously, tilting my feet and frantically feeling for solid ground, black water slapping my chin. Suddenly my feet touch something firm and I lunge forward, forcing my aching legs through the sludge.

Finally I stumble into a bed of reeds and up onto a bank covered in moss. And collapse. Swamp slop clogs my nostrils and as I snort it out my ears pop and black mucus dangles from my nose.

My cold and filthy clothes cling to my skin and my legs jerk uncontrollably. I rip the T-shirt from my head and splat the few mosquitoes still drilling into my face, then lie on my back for a minute or two, shivering but triumphant, high on relief. I made it! And I can hear the river.

As soon as my legs stop shaking I feel an itch in the crook of my left knee and stretch my hand down to scratch it, and touch a squidgy bulge beneath my jeans. Fingers trembling, I stand and undo my jeans, slowly pushing them down, dreading what I might find.

My heavy jeans drop to my ankles and I step out of them. I twist my leg and look down, and my worst fears are confirmed. The black bulge nestling in my knee looks like a slug but is something far worse. A leech. A slimy fat parasite, chewing my flesh and stealing my blood.

I reach down and try to flick it from my leg but it simply contracts and clings on tighter, continuing to feed. So I pinch its bloated body between my fingers as tightly as I can, and pull, stretching it like a stick of liquorice until it snaps off and writhes in the palm of my hand, puking blood.

More blood seeps from the puncture wound on my leg and I stare at the repulsive creature squirming in my hand, trying to latch onto my thumb; I pull my arm back and fling it as far as I can into the swamp and turn to a second one, dangling from my thigh. I tear this one off as well, and send it the same way as the first. Only then do I notice yet another one, clamped on my ankle.

As I bend to reach it I feel a lump in my pants, and I realise another leech is nestled between my buttocks.

I clench my cheeks together as hard as I can to try to crush it but the leech just squishes under the pressure and to my alarm it seems to slither even further up my bum. The thought of this blood-sucking parasite crawling up inside me is too horrific to bear. As I feel its sticky body pulsing, something snaps in my head. I've had enough!

Enough of the bloodsuckers. Enough of the heat, the humidity, the hunger. The stings, bites and cuts. The fear and exhaustion.

I step out of my pants, slide my slimy fingers between my buttocks and tear the leech away. The parasite had started to feed and I cry with pain as its teeth tear my skin and I can feel blood warm and wet on my cheeks. My blood!

Hatred burns through me. I won't be returning this one to the swamp alive. I want it to suffer like I'm suffering. I want revenge.

There's a flat rock nearby. I place the leech on it and before the creature can slither away I grab my trainer and splatter it. The leech splits open and sprays me with blood. I grin, and quickly tear the other one from my ankle. This one suffers the same fate and I laugh as it bursts with a loud pop. Naked, filthy and leaking blood, I search my lower body for more leeches and for a moment I'm more disappointed than relieved when I find none.

Killing spree over, the adrenaline drains from my body and my legs start to shake. Time to go.

My jeans are sodden and slimy but I need their protection so I pull them on, followed by my blackened socks and trainers, and with one last look of disgust at the swamp, I hitch my jeans up as far as I dare and head towards the sounds of the river.

EIGHT

Pears? No. Plums? No. Papayas! That's it!

Mouth drooling, I stare at the juicy fruit hanging from the tree before me. The strange fruit I'd never even considered trying before this trip. The fruit I was amazed to find I loved the taste of. It seems my luck has changed at last. The river is loud in my ears, but impatient as I am to reach it, I'm far too hungry to pass the fruit tree by.

I jump and try to grab a plump papaya but it's a pathetic attempt. I barely leave the ground and the fruit remains tantalisingly just out of reach. I grab a fallen branch and after half a dozen swipes I connect with my target and the papaya falls to the ground. I pounce on it, rip a strip of skin off with my teeth and bite into the soft orange flesh. The pulp is sweet and succulent and a stream of juice dribbles down my chin. I eagerly tear more skin off and keep biting and gulping down the chunks of flesh, spitting out the black seeds while I scrabble around, eagerly searching for any fallen fruit. But all I find are a few rotten ones, infested with worms and earwigs.

Leaves rustle high in the tree and I look up to see a black furry face peering down at me. The face disappears and reappears lower down, where the branches are thinner, and I can tell it's some sort of monkey. I like monkeys, always have, and I stay crouched and still, hoping he will move even closer. The leaves part and he swings down to squat on a low-hanging branch, hooting quietly and staring at me. His boldness surprises me but I'm not frightened, instead I'm glad of his company.

Absentmindedly scratching his belly, the monkey continues to stare. Then his mouth opens wide and his lips curl into what I decide is a smile, so I pick a seed out from between my teeth and slowly stand and smile back at him, to let him know I mean him no harm.

His musky scent wafts over me. He smells like a wet dog with BO and I instinctively sniff my own armpit and recoil at the stink. The monkey copies me, lifting his arm to sniff his own pit and grimace, and I laugh, but a darkening sky and the sound of the river nearby remind me I have no time for games, and I break eye contact and resume my search for fruit to take with me.

I've been looking for no more than a minute or so with no luck when a soft thud close by interrupts my search. I stand and take two steps towards it and see a small papaya, green and unripe, lying on the ground, its stalk and two leaves still attached. Curious, I look up to see where the fruit has come from and there is the monkey, staring down at me, but now he is grinning and juggling another green papaya in his hands. I smile, and give a little nod of my head to thank him. OK, so the fruit is unripe and inedible, but with a little encouragement from me perhaps my new friend will pick some more, and I'll be able to eat the next one.

I turn to continue my search but as I do I feel a thump in the small of my back and another green papaya bounces onto the ground and rolls away. I rub the base of my spine and swivel around to glare at the monkey... and pause.

The monkey is no longer alone. He's been joined by two others, both considerably bigger than he is, and they appear to be scolding my new friend, slapping him around the head and pointing angrily in my direction.

I stand and as I do so one of the newcomers snatches a papaya from the first monkey and throws it at me. His aim is surprisingly good and I have to duck to prevent the fruit hitting me in the face. I stare at the monkey in surprise, only to see him fling his hands high above his head and dance along the bough, hooting and thumping his chest. His behaviour is quickly copied by his companion, and now even the first monkey joins in, all three screeching abuse at me.

Only now, with more monkeys arriving every second do I realise how badly I have misread the situation. I thought the monkey wanted to be friends, to help me even. But I was wrong. He never wanted to be my friend. These apes aren't trying to help me. They're warning me off. This tree is theirs. Its fruit belongs to them, and they aren't about to share it with any other creature, least of all a ground-living, tailless one.

Papayas, twigs and branches rain down on me. I don't do confrontation, so I take a step backwards and turn to leave, but as I do so a sharp branch whips across the back of my neck, stinging my sunburnt skin. Triumphant hoots fill the air and I can feel my cheeks burning with the realisation that I am being bullied. Again. I grab a green papaya, spin round, take aim and throw it as hard as I can, grunting with satisfaction as it hits my target smack in the middle of his chest. The monkey's hooting stops. He parts his wiry hair and rubs the spot where the papaya made contact. Then he glares down at me and howls with rage, jumping up and down, pulling his hair and working himself into a frenzy.

The mood has turned really nasty now and the tree shakes with the fury of a howling mob of monkeys all screaming abuse. I am seriously outnumbered.

I turn to leave but a turd hits my shoulder and splatters across my cheek. At first I can't comprehend what has happened, it's too gross, too disgusting to believe. But then the stink hits me, a sort of sour milk and farts smell. I stare at the monkeys bouncing above me and all thoughts of retreat evaporate.

I'm beyond angry, incensed by my humiliation and the hail of fruit and poo raining down on me, and it's my turn to rant and rave. I use my T-shirt to wipe the mess from my face, pick up a stick and scream at my assailants.

'Come on then! Come on! Is that all you've got?'

But my challenge only serves to spur them on and within seconds I am pelted with a barrage of fruit and branches. Burning with rage I hurl my stick at them and scramble around, searching for ammunition, and blindly chuck papayas and sticks into the tree. The noise is deafening, there must be at least thirty jeering apes chucking poo and whatever they can rip from the tree down at me.

I kick a pile of leaves aside and find a stone, oval and heavy, the perfect size for my hand. I toss it in the air, judging its weight, while selecting my target – a grinning monkey with his arm cocked ready to launch something at me. I take aim and throw the stone as hard as I can. It whizzes through the air and smacks into the monkey's forehead. Bull's-eye! His head snaps back. A papaya drops from his hand and he grabs his head and whimpers with pain.

I whoop and punch the air then give him the finger. The rain of missiles slows, then stops completely; the noise abates as the monkeys stare at their wounded comrade, then down at me. I glare back at them, square my shoulders and stand as tall as I can, and thump my chest, letting them know I am up for a fight and there is plenty more where that came from.

But it's clear the monkeys are far from intimidated, and I am now facing the deadly hate of an enraged mob.

One monkey, bolder than the rest, hangs by one arm from the lowest branch and drops to the ground, landing solidly on all fours, gnashing his teeth and glaring at me.

My sense of triumph evaporates. Exhausted as I am, if the mob decides to attack there is no way I can outrun them or fight them all. I have to get out of here before more monkeys join their companion. Mind racing, I vaguely remember reading somewhere that attack is supposed to be the best form of defence, and with the monkey now advancing towards me I can't think of anything else to do, so I charge at him, yelling and waving my arms, and to my relief his eyes widen in surprise, and he drops his stick and turns and scrambles back up the tree trunk.

In that instant I turn and run. As fast as I can. Charging blindly through the undergrowth, unable to see where I'm going and not daring to look behind.

I've covered no more than a hundred metres or so when I suddenly burst out from the trees into bright sunlight, and the earth falls away beneath me.

NINE

I tumble down the steep slope, rolling over and over, desperately trying to grab hold of something to slow my fall. Thorns tear my skin and a sharp pain shoots up my arm as I hit something solid and come to a juddering halt. I lie still for a moment, chest heaving, with a loud rumbling noise in my ears. For a moment I assume it's the sound of my heavy breathing, but as my head clears I realise it is the river I can hear, and by the sound of it I am only a few metres away.

Rubbing my throbbing elbow, I look down at the thing which halted my fall. It's a sheet of white metal about the size of a pillow, heat blistered and streaked with fuel stains. I've found the plane!

Dizzy but elated I climb to my feet and eagerly look around. I can see the plane's cockpit wedged against a sandbar in the middle of the river, no more than ten metres away.

'Dad! Dad!' I shout over and over, and listen hard, straining for a reply. But I hear nothing above the sounds of the river, and the cries of vultures circling overhead.

Vultures! Perhaps Dad's injured and unconscious, somewhere on the sandbar.

I run to the river and wade in, eyes scanning for any sign of him.

Halfway across, the riverbed falls away and a strong current pulls at my legs. I brace myself against it and keep going, thankful my life jacket survived the fall. A purple and blue fuel slick coats the water around the sandbar and stings the cuts and scratches on my arms, but I hardly feel it, I'm too focused on reaching the plane.

I clamber onto the sandbar and only now can I hear a faint humming sound above the noise of the river, and my heart jumps as I think it could be the radio. The noise grows louder as I approach the cockpit and a new smell fills my nostrils. A meaty, smoky smell. An odour I vaguely recognise but can't identify. I reach the cockpit. Peering within all I can see is darkness and a whirling mass of flies. I bang hard on the metal and duck as a torrent of flies streams out through the shattered windscreen.

The pilot's body is still strapped in his seat, head snapped backwards. Maggots crawl over his eyeless face, and he smells like a barbecue.

I turn away and heave, spewing up stinging orange bile and the small amount of papaya flesh I had managed to consume. I wipe my mouth on the back of my hand. I have never seen a dead body before, or smelt one, and it's gruesome.

But at least it's not Dad.

I try to remember the pilot's name, and I can't. All I can remember about him is his cool Aviator sunglasses, and his skull-and-crossbones Zippo lighter, the one the wind couldn't blow out when he rolled and smoked a cigarette just before we took off. The practical part of my mind says I should search him for his sunglasses and the lighter, and any other useful things. But the thought of touching his charred flesh makes the bile rise back up my throat, and I decide it's too dark. I'll do it in the morning. Then I'll bury him. Or at least that's what I tell myself.

I take a quick look around the cockpit, hoping to spot a torch, or signal flares, or anything to eat, but it's too dark to see, and the flies have returned.

I really want to find my rucksack, with its can of Coke, the chocolate and chewing gum, and my phone. But dark clouds are massing overhead, the light is fading fast and however much I want my stuff, I'm not prepared to grope around the wreckage in the dark. I have to get back to shore before the storm hits and the sun sets and the caimans emerge.

A quick scan around the sandbar reveals no sign of Dad, no footsteps or other clues as to where he might be. I cup my hands and call, 'Dad!' again and again, but there's no reply.

Rain starts to fall. Hard and fast, rebounding off the water into my eyes and reducing visibility. And with the current now stronger, it takes me much longer to wade back to shore, fearfully squinting through the deluge for any sign of caimans.

I clamber up the slippery bank and try to find some shelter, but it's impossible to see anything much in the dark and driving rain. Then I remember the metal sheet and wrench it from the bushes and try to use it as an umbrella, but each time I lift it above my head the wind howls beneath it and threatens to tear it from my grasp.

A sudden powerful gust eventually rips the sheet from my icy fingers and, left with no protection at all, the hard rain stabs my face like meat skewers. I wrap my arms over my head and squeeze my eyes shut, trying to block out the storm, but I can't. It's too loud, and I'm too cold and scared.

For hour after torturous hour the storm rages. Stabbing, relentless rain hammers my shivering body and churns the ground to mud. Booming claps of thunder shake the air and echo off the ravine walls.

All is darkness except when bolts of lightning slice the sky and illuminate the raging river, its surface whipped to foam. Each time it happens I can see the river is far higher and closer than before, and I climb further up the slope and crouch down among the bushes.

Sometime in the early hours, with the storm at its fiercest, and a howling gale threatening to pluck me from my perch and fling me into the river, I hear a new sound, a growling, menacing roar, like a monstrous creature being held against its will. It's beyond loud, beyond deafening. And it's raw, primeval and thick with threat.

The roar intensifies, drowning out the storm, and I hug my knees tight against my chest and shake uncontrollably. I'm hysterical now. Beyond reason. The river has come alive, I'm sure of it, and it's coming for me.

I have to get away. I try to climb higher up the slope but I lose my footing and slip in the mud, and as the icy wind hits my bare foot I realise I have stepped out of a trainer. A flash of lightning illuminates the slope below me just long enough for me to glimpse my trainer floating away in a stream of liquid mud. In a few seconds it will be in the river. I can't lose it! I have to get it back. I grab the base of a thorn bush to lower myself down.

And the wave hits. A wall of water thunders down the ravine in a grinding roar, funnelled by the sloping walls, tearing up trees and bushes. The crest of the wave claws at my legs and threatens to sweep me away. I grip the bush with both hands as tightly as I can and hang on as the water pummels my legs. A metallic groaning noise joins the roar, and I scream.

Then as swiftly as it arrived, the flash flood passes. I raise my head.

One lightning-lit glance is enough to tell me my trainer has gone.

And so has the plane.

TEN

Steam rises from my T-shirt, the sun warm on my back.

The river is flowing much higher and faster than yesterday, dark brown and lumpy with uprooted trees and bushes. The sandbar is deep below water and there's no trace of the plane.

Or Dad.

I'm gutted. I was so sure I would find him. But the vultures have moved on. They must have been here for the pilot. Dad has to be alive. He's either searching for me somewhere else or a rescue team has already found him. It's the only logical explanation. For all I know, Dad and the search team could be at my sandspit right now! I have to get back. There's no point in staying here. There's no food. No shelter. No stream for fresh water, and another flash flood could kill me. And with all traces of the plane gone and the ravine's steep walls hampering visibility, a helicopter could fly directly overhead and not see me. I have a far better chance of being found at my beach, with its open sky and my *HELP* sign.

But how will I get there? My legs ache, my elbow is swollen and stiff and even if I still had both trainers the ravine walls are too steep and slippery to climb with only one good arm. If I did somehow reach the top the monkeys could be waiting, and I would have to cross the swamp.

I'll have to swim back.

But impatient as I am to get going, I'm in no hurry to enter the water. Even if my arm was 100%, I'm not a strong swimmer, and the river's flowing far too fast for me to risk it at the moment. I'll have to wait for the level to drop. In the meantime I might as well search for my trainer and something to eat.

I retie the life-jacket strings and clamber along the side of the slope, just above the flash-flood mark, checking piles of flotsam for my trainer. It's hard to keep my footing on the steep bank, and after an hour or more of fruitless searching I'm hot and filthy and plagued by tiny black flies. I'm about to give up when I see a pile of debris snagged in the branches of an uprooted tree, a little further downstream. Then with a sigh of relief I spot the bright neon stripes on my trainer bobbing amongst it.

I wade out to the debris and grab my shoe. I'm about to shuffle back to shore when I catch sight of something glinting just below the surface further out, swaying in spindly branches bent by the current. Something small and metallic. Most probably a piece of scrap metal from the plane. But what if it's something valuable to me – a torch, or a water bottle? Or even the pilot's lighter!

The object is another couple of metres further out into the river, and I will have to go out of my depth to reach it. I hesitate. It's too risky. But then again the possibility of being able to carry water, or see in the dark, or best of all light a fire, is too tempting to resist.

I put my trainer on and slowly work my way along the flimsy dam and out into the river, pausing each time the tree creaks and shifts in the current. Its roots are working loose from the bank and with any more pressure from me it could tear free completely. But my mind's made up. I'm only an arm's length away from the object now and determined to reach it. I shuffle a little further out and as I take a last step I'm swept into the middle of the tangled branches and only the life jacket prevents me from being dragged under.

The tree creaks again, and groans, and I feel it shift further and sway. I have to hurry. Taking a deep breath, I dunk my face in the water and grope around. I feel the object, cold and hard, and as my fingers close around it, the tree's roots pull free. The tree is claimed by the current.

I wrap my arms around the trunk and hang on, legs dangling. But just before I do, I manage to catch a glimpse of the object clasped tightly in my hand.

It's not a torch, or a water bottle, or the pilot's lighter.

It's a watch. Dad's watch. Badly dented and covered in deep scratches and indentations which look just like teeth marks. Caiman teeth.

ELEVEN

With the river flowing so fast, I reach the rapids above my sandspit before noon.

The first part of the trip was by far the most frightening, with the tree ricocheting off the ravine walls and bucking wildly in the current. But somehow I managed to hold on until the walls fell away and the river widened and slowed. The tree then proved to be a pretty good raft and the rest of the ride was uneventful until I hit the rapids and had to walk the last few hundred metres.

The flood mark on the beach is higher than before and the sudden surge has washed away half of my *HELP* sign. But there are no hints that another human being has been here.

Yesterday I was sure I must have fought my way through many miles of jungle to reach the crash site, but it turns out that the plane came down no more than a mile or so upriver from here. If I'd followed the river's course rather than heading into the jungle then not only would I have avoided the swamp and the monkeys but I would have reached the wreckage in a fraction of the time. Hours earlier in fact. More than early enough to retrieve my rucksack and any other useful items I could find, and with plenty of time to search the surrounding area in daylight, before the storm hit. It's a devastating thought and I dunk my head in the stream to try to wash my bitterness away, swearing I'll never enter the jungle again.

I drink long and deep from the stream before scanning the river for any sign of the otters. Nothing. I walk back to the shade of the giant tree and hug the trunk, thankful to be back. I take my time removing my socks and trainers from my bruised and blistered feet and place them in the sun to dry before taking a closer look at Dad's watch.

Apart from a few dents and gouges it appears to be intact and, holding my breath, I pull the small crown out and wind it. The second hand starts to click immediately and I breathe a huge sigh of relief. The watch is tough, really tough. Like Dad. It's a good sign. And I have a sudden cheering thought – as long as the watch works then Dad must still be alive. All I have to do is keep it ticking. With the sun now directly overhead I set the time to twelve o'clock before turning the watch over and tracing the gouges on the casing which on first sight I thought were tooth marks. But on closer inspection I decide I was overreacting and they're nothing more than scratches and chips caused by the crash.

The watch is far too big and heavy for my wrist and I won't risk losing it or damaging it any further, so I give the glass a final polish before tucking it into a pocket in the life jacket and securing the Velcro.

I yawn and stretch, and rub my elbow. I should rebuild my *HELP* sign, and check the beach to see if the flood has left anything edible behind. But I haven't had a moment's rest since leaving to search for the plane yesterday morning, and hardly any sleep since the night of the crash. Now safely back in the shade of my giant tree, exhaustion overwhelms me. I place the life jacket under my head and close my eyes.

A bark wakes me. Then whistles. The otters! I jump to my feet. The sun is low in the sky and a warm breeze stirs the trees. Another bark and I run towards the river.

I have a raging thirst but a drink can wait. I want to see the otters first. Slowing down as I approach the bend, I see the mother and pup swimming close to Otter Rock, and trembling with excitement I sit down to watch them.

My intention is to stay for five minutes at most, before quenching my thirst and searching for something to eat but it's so good to see them, and they're so entertaining, so full of life, that before I know it half an hour has passed, or it could be an hour or more, I don't know. But I do know that in this time the mother catches two crabs, three catfish and five piranhas. The piranhas are clearly the pup's favourite, and he squeaks and whistles with pleasure as he grasps each one firmly between his paws and attacks the head first, crunching and grunting until only the jaws and tail remain. Why he takes such delight in wolfing down the piranhas I don't know. Perhaps one bit him when he was younger, or their flashy red bellies annoy him. Or perhaps they just taste the best!

The mother spends an incredible amount of time underwater, and after she's caught fish number five I decide to time her. I don't have Dad's watch with me so I count elephants instead, and amass a herd of three hundred and six for one of her dives, which I work out to mean she's held her breath for five minutes. Five minutes! I managed a piddling thirty-two seconds once, and that was while clinging to the ladder in the shallow end of the swimming pool.

But by the time she's caught her eighth fish I'm seriously envious again and once more I think about swimming across the river to steal one, even though I know it's a ridiculous idea. She and her pup would be gone long before I got anywhere near them, and as hungry as I am I will not risk scaring them away. So I stay and watch, making the most of their presence while growing more jealous by the second, until the otters finally depart and I rise and head for the stream.

By the time I return to camp I'm in a seriously bad mood. I have no food. No fire for warmth and light, or cooking. No smoke to act as a signal to search planes and provide protection from mosquitoes. My sleeping area is a tick-infested mess. I'm a mess. Septic bites and scabby scratches crisscross my sunburnt, peeling skin. My filthy clothes emit a pungent, damp aroma, like PE kit left in the bag to ferment. My head aches continuously. And every hour I don't eat I grow weaker.

Enough! If I'm to stand any chance of living long enough for a rescue party to find me then something has to change. I have to change. No more wallowing in self-pity. No more simply waiting for things to get better. No more laziness.

I've got to get off my arse and do something. I've got to take responsibility for myself. Everything I do from this moment on has to be with only one aim in mind – to survive.

But how do I begin?

What would Dad do? He'd 'take stock and prioritise', that's what he'd do. So that's what I'll do. I'll make a list of everything I have and then I can decide what's missing. What don't I have that's most vital for my survival?

Well, I do have a steady supply of fresh water from the stream, and shade from the midday sun, and a location that's visible from the air. I have a life jacket, jeans, T-shirt, pants, socks and trainers, and Dad's watch.

So what do I need the most that I don't have?

Food. Sleep. Fire.

Now to prioritise. What do I need most urgently? Food.

But there's a problem. After what happened when I went searching for the plane I can't face the prospect of entering the jungle to look for fruit, and I can't just rely on the river to wash it up. I don't have the guts to handle raw grubs and snails. I need to be able to cook it and to do that I need a fire. The smoke will also keep the mosquitoes at bay, and signal my location. Fire first then.

Decision made, I feel a bit better, a little stronger. More positive. But it's too late to do anything today. I'll try to rest now and start first thing in the morning.

Tomorrow will be different. Tomorrow I'll do something to help myself, no matter how hard it might be.

Tomorrow I will create fire.

TWELVE

To my surprise it's light when I wake. My exhaustion must have caught up with me.

I yell, 'Hello,' and 'Help!' five or six times, not really expecting a reply. Then I jog to the stream, keen to get started.

I take a quick drink and peer hopefully across the river at Otter Rock. No otters.

Time to get on with things. Time to light a fire. But how? I have no matches. No lighter. Nothing.

It seemed such a simple idea last night. Such a straightforward and logical one. Well it doesn't seem so simple now... I try to remember how Bear Grylls did it. He didn't have any matches either, but I do remember one episode when he started a fire by banging two rocks together, really hard, and when he did sparks flew everywhere.

So I collect a dozen rocks, all different shapes and sizes, and excitedly bash them together, and after an hour or so I have a pile of rubble, gritty eyes, grazed and blistered hands, and not even a hint of a spark.

I glare at the shattered rocks but I'm not giving up. If anything, now I've actually started, I'm even more determined than ever to make this work. Another Bear Grylls episode comes to mind, when he used a stick about the size of a wooden spoon. From what I can remember I think he placed one end of it on a piece of bark and rubbed the stick backwards and forwards until the friction caused a spark. Or something like that. I can't recall all the details, but I figure I've remembered enough to give it a go.

Finding fuel for the fire is no problem. There are plenty of bits of bark, sticks and broken branches beneath my tree and washed up on the shore, and I soon have a wigwam of twigs to use as a starter fire and a pile of big sticks to add as soon as the fire is alight.

Now I need something to use as tinder. I reckon the grass stems and dead leaves I have been sleeping on might work, so I spread a handful out in the sun to dry while I go in search of a spinning stick.

This proves to be much harder but for once I don't retreat to the shade to doze through the midday heat, instead I keep searching. But every stick I find is too short, or too thin. Or too bent. Or knobbly. Too soft or too brittle, and it bends or snaps as soon as I put any pressure on it.

By mid-afternoon I'm seriously fed up. My hands are bruised and bleeding. My head is pounding. The back of my neck and my arms are on fire and I decide to take a dip in the river to cool down and try to clear my head. In too much of a hurry to bother looking where I'm going, I trip over my *HELP* sign on the way, scattering the 'P', and there it is! Standing upright in the sand; an ideal spinning stick, just the right length and as thick as a whiteboard marker pen, with no prominent knots or knobbly bits. Perfect!

At last I have everything I need. I grab the stick and run back up the beach. The river can wait.

Placing a strip of bark close to my twig wigwam, I sprinkle a handful of ripped leaves and grass stems on the bark to act as tinder. Then I take a deep breath and try to contain my excitement, place one end of the stick in the middle of the leaves and begin to rub it backwards and forwards between my palms as fast as I can.

The stick immediately shoots out through my fingertips. I retrieve it and start again. This time it skates to the left, upending the bark and scattering the leaves. I grunt, gather the tinder and try again, pressing down harder this time, but as soon as I put any pressure on the stick and start to spin it, the tip just skids off the bark, and after a few more tries the end of the stick is not even warm. In fact the only heat generated appears to be coming from a burning sensation across my palms and the temper rising up my chest.

'Damn!'

I've obviously got something wrong. Think! What am I missing here? Got it! I need to find a way to keep the tip in one place. To anchor it. Turning the bark over, I see a flaky knot, halfway along, about twice the circumference of the stick, and I use a splinter of rock to dig it out, creating a circular trough for the stick's tip.

On my next attempt the stick stays in the trough and the tip definitely warms up, but there's no smoke, and no indication that the tinder will ignite.

Something still isn't right. I try to recall what else Bear did, what have I forgotten? And I remember – sand! Bear put sand grains in the dent to increase the friction. I grin, at least this bit will be easy. I have more than enough sand!

I drop a pinch of sand in the trough and start spinning the stick again, ignoring the painful blisters ballooning on my palms. The stick is much harder to turn. I can feel the increased resistance along my fingers, and I can hear the sand grains grating the bark.

As I adjust the pressure and speed to spin the stick more efficiently, a tiny wisp of grey smoke curls up from the trough. Then another, and I'm sure I can smell burning. 'Yes!' I've done it!

I drop the stick and lift the bark with its smouldering cargo to my lips and blow, to feed the ember. And I blow the tinder clean off the bark and onto the sand.

I clench my fists, breathe deeply and try again, and the grass starts to smoke, but as soon as I lift the bark, the straw and leaves scatter in the breeze.

I jam the bark into the sand and try to figure out what to do. The stick's working well enough but the straw is too light, too flimsy, and the leaves won't catch. I need a different material to bulk up the straw, something just as flammable, but heavier. And I have to be more patient, something I've never been good at. I have to keep spinning and wait until the tinder is well and truly alight before trying to transfer it.

I walk the shoreline, scanning for any suitable material, hands jammed in pockets to prevent me gnawing my bloody cuticles, rolling bits of tissue paper between my fingers. And then I realise! My pockets are full of scraps of chewing-gum wrappers, cotton thread and tissue paper, and although they've been saturated in the swamp and the river, they're dry now and might just work. I empty my pockets, mix the assorted fluff with the grass stems, and place my new, improved tinder in the trough, along with another pinch of sand.

Stick poised, I squint at Dad's watch and track the second hand's stuttered progress around the dial. As soon it touches twelve I start to spin, slowly and deliberately moving the stick to and fro, gradually increasing the speed until, after twenty-five seconds, the first wisp of smoke curls up from the trough. My arms and shoulders ache and my hands sting, but this time I fight the urge to stop and remove the stick too soon. I told myself I'd keep spinning for a full minute to give the new tinder a chance to catch fire properly this time, no matter how much it hurts.

Another glance at Dad's watch. Thirty-five seconds, more tendrils of smoke, thicker now, weaving together.

At forty-five seconds I'm sure I can see a glowing ember. The temptation to stop and transfer the tinder into the stick wigwam is overwhelming but I resist. I check the watch, fifty-six seconds. Just a few seconds more...

What was that – a flame? A flame! That's never happened before!

Sixty seconds. I remove the stick and bend forward to pick up the bark. And a fat dollop of sweat falls from the tip of my nose and splatters directly into the dent, extinguishing the tiny flame. I blink, and stare in disbelief at the globule of sooty sweat filling the crater.

I leap to my feet and scream, and jump up and down on the bark, burying it deep in the sand. Then I boot the twig wigwam high in the air, and grab the spinning stick in both hands and before I can stop myself I raise my leg and bring the stick down hard on my knee, snapping it in two.

Shaking with anger I am only vaguely aware of what I have done, but I do know I need to cool down before I lose it completely and injure myself. I stomp to the river, wade in waist deep and thrust my head under, holding it there as long as I can, until the need to breathe is stronger than my anger.

I've achieved nothing. All I've done is waste valuable energy and confirm I'm no Bear Grylls. I am whatever the opposite of Bear Grylls is. I am pathetic.

I sit in the water for five minutes or so, shoulders slumped, disgusted with myself for losing it and snapping the stick. Eventually I've cooled down enough to start worrying about piranhas and caimans, and I leave the river and walk back to my tree.

My failure, and missing my midday sleep, have completely drained me and I'm too fed up to even consider trying to do anything else. There's no point. I'd only fail. I decide to have a lie down and reach into the life-jacket pocket to check the time on Dad's watch.

It's not there.

I have left it out on the sand, beside the big sticks. Great! I hobble out onto the beach and quickly grab it. And immediately drop it again, crying out in pain. The watch is red hot, and I'm an idiot.

The watch thuds into the sand, glass face up and tilted, reflecting the sun directly into my eyes, blinding me. Shielding my eyes, I take my top off, grope for the watch and wrap it inside the T-shirt. I stumble back to the shade, shoulders slumped, sucking my burnt fingers and blinking back tears.

THIRTEEN

Two hours have passed since sunrise and I'm still no closer to finding the guts to do what I have to.

The idea came to me sometime during a restless night, when I remembered how the beam of light from Dad's watch blinded me and I realised that the glass can focus not only light, but heat as well. I turn the watch over and over in my hand, tracing every scratch and dent with my fingertips, searching for more reasons to justify doing what I know I must. For the thousandth time I go over the list in my head – the watch is really old and worth nothing. It's badly scratched and dented and most of the silver plate has been rubbed away. It's ridiculously heavy and the ancient metal strap is clunky and far too big for my wrist, and I don't even know if it tells the correct time.

And I've decided I don't need to know what the time is anyway. In fact, knowing how many long hours have passed since I last ate, or how few are left until nightfall, is not comforting or of any use whatsoever. It sucks. And it doesn't matter. All that matters is I keep believing that sometime soon the rescue party will find me, and I have to do whatever it takes to stay alive until they do. That's what I keep telling myself anyway. But I know that this watch, this battered, beaten-up piece of metal is far more than just a means of telling the time. It's Dad's watch. One of his most prized possessions. It belonged to Grandpa, and Gran gave it to Dad the day Grandpa died. And however much I want to deny it, or how ridiculous it is, I know what I said. I said that as long as the watch is working then Dad must be alive.

And now I want to destroy it.

I shove the watch back in my pocket and squeeze my fist within the other one until my jagged fingernails scrape the scab off my knuckle and it starts to bleed.

What am I thinking? It's insane! A stupid idea that almost certainly won't work, and when it doesn't I will have to live with what I've done.

But still the voice whispers in my ear, telling me I've run out of options. Telling me the only thing I can be certain of is that without a fire I'm going to die. Last night was the coldest yet. Without food and warmth I won't survive much longer.

I can't! I just can't. And I won't.

But I have to.

I stay rooted in the shade of the giant tree through midday, trying to make my mind up one way or the other, not even allowing myself the relief of walking to the stream for a drink.

Then at three o'clock on the dot, my thirst and fear of the coming cold and dark night finally persuades me, and I stand. I have to try. I have to do this. I have to make this work. I have no choice.

Even though the sun is dropping rapidly I take my time collecting all the bits I need for the fire, discarding anything that isn't ideal. Half-submerged in silt by the mouth of the stream, I even find a hollowed-out log which might work as a cooking pot. But I leave it where it is. As positive as I'm trying to be I won't tempt fate by getting ahead of myself.

By four-thirty I have everything I need – a heavy, sharp-edged stone to use as a hammer. A flattish rock to rest the watch on. My strip of bark. An egg-sized bale of fluff and straw, and a bundle of twigs for kindling.

My new wigwam construction is much better than the previous one. Sturdier, with interlocking sticks and a gap wide enough to be able to insert the bark without having to tip it.

I pick up the watch and daub a fingertip of mud on the spot where I must strike – the only possible weakness I could find, a slight bulge in the seal where the glass face meets the body.

Everything is ready. I can delay no longer.

'I'm sorry, Dad,' I say. 'I'm so, so sorry, Grandpa.'

I raise my stone hammer level with my eyes and bring its sharp edge down on the mud spot as hard as I can.

One blow is all it takes. The stone strikes the watch at the exact spot I've marked, the glass springs free and the metal casing bucks and slides from the rock. The glass lies face down in the sand, in one piece, and the metal body appears to still be intact as well, with the dial and hands still connected.

I sink to my knees. I can't believe it's worked. Part One has actually worked and I haven't destroyed the watch! I scoop up the metal body and run back to my tree. After carefully tucking the watch back into the pocket of the life jacket, I return to the beach and polish the glass face on my T-shirt, over and over, until it gleams in the sun. Then, kneeling next to the bark, I balance the glass between my trembling thumb and forefinger, just above the tinder, directly in line with the sun's rays, and tilt it.

This is it. The moment of truth.

I lean forward and move the glass in and out, adjusting the tilt until a bright yellow dot shivers across the bark and comes to rest in the centre of my straw and fluff ball.

The dot starts to smoulder and turns black almost immediately. Far quicker than I expected or dared hope. Tendrils of smoke curl up from the fluff and the black spot expands until it's the size of a five-pence piece. Right in the centre of the circle something starts to glow. I drop to my stomach and gently blow across the bark, eyes fixed on the glowing ember in the centre of the tinder ball, pleading with it to ignite. Another cloud blots the sun and I glance up in alarm to see the sky is now more grey than blue. I blow a little harder, struggling to control my exhalations to feed the ember without blowing it out.

Something flickers. I squint. Flames. I see flames! I blow again and suddenly my tinder ball bursts into glorious flame. I lift my bark with its precious cargo and insert it into the base of the wigwam. And blow. Each time I exhale, the tinder ball pulses red and gold, and flames claw up towards the twigs, groping for a hold. But the ball is unravelling fast and the tissues and straw are being consumed at an alarming rate.

Heart racing, I blow again, aiming for where the flames seem strongest. One yellow finger reaches higher than the rest, and jabs a twig. The twig catches fire. So does the one next to it, and faster than my eyes can follow, the flames fan out and climb and spread until the entire wigwam is alight. With shaking hands I quickly add more twigs, then sticks, then branches, until I have a magnificent, blazing fire, spitting and cracking and radiating so much heat I have to shuffle back a few metres. I wipe my brow and stare at the fire in amazement, grinning like an idiot and blaming my blinking, watery eyes on the smoke.

I can't believe it. I've done it. I've actually done it. I've made fire.

I've made fire!

I leap to my feet and dance around my creation, my flaming miracle, whooping and hollering. I'm too weak to stay on my feet for long and I fall over, and lie on my back, laughing and kicking my legs in the air like a dying fly. I must look ridiculous but I don't care, something is coursing through my veins and drenching my brain with a rush of relief and accomplishment, and the feeling is too powerful to keep bottled up inside.

It's the most intense blast of joy and achievement I've ever felt.

A sizzling sound comes from the flames as some sort of insect is incinerated and as the cooking scent wafts up my nose it triggers an instant and overpowering response in my mind, reminding me how painfully hungry I am.

The wooden bowl! The snails! I dig the log out of the silt and quickly wash it, then run to the end of the sandspit and peel a dozen yellow snails off the rocks to drop into it.

On the way back I fill the bowl with fresh water from the stream, then hurry to the fire and wedge the anvil rock amongst glowing branches near the edge. I rest the bowl on top of it, hoping it doesn't leak or catch fire. Thankfully the bowl appears to be waterproof or too wet to burn. The water boils, a grey scum appears on the surface and slime clings to the edges, and as the level drops my nostrils fill with a disgusting smell. Normally this would be more than enough to make me gag and run a mile, but I'm too hungry to be choosy; my body needs food too much.

So I breathe through my mouth instead, and stir the murky water, listening to the snail shells clinking together, and the hiss of spilled water as it slops into the flames. After a couple of minutes I figure they must be cooked so I pull the bowl clear of the flames and upend it, and the now dark brown snails tumble onto the ground.

I tap a steaming snail with my stone hammer. The shell cracks to reveal a lump of grey flesh and I can feel my mouth filling with saliva. After a hurried attempt to peel off the biggest bits of shell I put the snail in my mouth and chew. At first taste it seems to be more gritty shell than meat but the texture is not unlike chewing gum, and even with the fragments of shell pricking my tongue it's not completely inedible. I swallow and wait, head tilted back.

The snail stays down, and the rest quickly follow the first.

Sometime later, shortly after sunset, I lie on my back with my hands supporting my head, basking in the warmth of my fire, burping loudly.

Cracked snail shells litter the ground. I don't know how many trips I made to Snail Rock to fill my bowl, or how many I ate in total, but my belly is as round as a beach ball, and I'm grinning.

Snails. I've eaten snails!

OK, so they're repeating on me and bits of shell are lodged between my teeth, but I've had no cramp attacks since the snail binge and I haven't vomited any back up. Result!

I peer at Dad's watch. The hands are stuck at four thirty-seven, when the rock struck and I've lost the crown so I can't wind it. But I don't feel guilty. I'm sure it can be fixed. It's just on standby really. And I know Dad would have done the same. I place it back in the pocket of the life jacket along with the glass and fasten the seal, and although I'll miss the comfort of using the jacket as a pillow, I won't risk damaging the watch any further so I carry the jacket to the giant tree and wedge it firmly in the lower branches before returning to the fire.

Pinpricks of reflected light speckle the blackness. Insects that would be biting and stinging me now without my fire to keep them at bay.

Holding my hands as close to the fire as I can bear, I gaze into the flames. It's been a long time since I felt this good. Yes, I'm still scared, and desperate to be rescued, but for the first time since the crash I don't feel completely helpless and lost. I feel warm. I feel full. I feel proud of myself.

I burp again, loudly and satisfyingly, and sip my hot water. God how I wish I had a teabag, or better still, a jar of hot chocolate!

I catch myself. I must not think negative thoughts. I must focus on what I do have, not what I don't. I have light and warmth from my fire, the means to boil water and cook, and smoke to keep the mosquitoes at bay. Tomorrow I will find a way to make the smoke even thicker to signal my position to the search teams. Then I will make a proper bed, and set myself chores like foraging for food, collecting firewood, washing myself and keeping my sleeping area clean. I will start a routine and stick to it. It won't be easy but I can do it. I know I can. After all, I made fire and I ate snails. I made fire! I ate snails! And if I can make fire and eat snails then I can do anything.

It's been a long and tiring day, but a good one. With a fire to get me through the night and more than enough to keep me busy during the day, the prospect of having to stay here for another day or two doesn't seem as bad as it did before.

I yawn, and stretch, and turn on my side, facing the fire, and just before I close my eyes I decide to give my giant tree, my shelter, a name. I decide to call it the 'Joshua Tree', after Dad's favourite album by U2. Mum says that if our house ever caught fire then *The Joshua Tree* is the one thing Dad would run back into the flames to save. That, and his watch.

FOURTEEN

Damn!

Despite being warm and dry I had a crap night's sleep. Whenever I did manage to fall asleep it was never for very long. I kept jolting awake, either from fear of the fire going out or a sudden panic attack that my fire was just a dream. My bloated stomach is as hard as a bowling ball and trying to sleep without the life jacket for a pillow has given me a cricked neck.

My plan for today was simple. Begin with a big breakfast of snails to give me energy for the day ahead. Check to see if the otters are around. Then start my chores by finding a way to create a thick smoke signal without smothering the fire.

But as I stumble around trying to find my wooden bowl, it's depressingly obvious that breakfast and smoke signals will have to wait. The fire is 90% ash.

I have next to no firewood left, and without more fuel I can't see it staying alight for more than an hour or two at most. The branches I collected yesterday are being consumed far too quickly, and if I am to avoid spending my entire time gathering firewood then I'll have to find some heavier, slower-burning logs.

Fortunately I do not have to search very long for the right logs, and find three suitable ones on the edge of the jungle no more than thirty paces away. They're more than a metre and with any luck should burn for a few hours at least. But they're also extremely thick and heavy. Too heavy to carry. I'll have to drag them back one at a time.

With head bowed I haul the first one out onto the beach, trying to keep my knees bent and my spine straight, like Dad taught me. But the log keeps sinking into the soft sand and by the time I'm halfway across, my back and shoulders are aching. Eventually, after much straining and swearing, I reach the fire, drenched in sweat, and although I know I should roll the log onto the glowing embers without delay, I'm too knackered. I leave it by the fire and collapse in the shade instead. But after a few minutes catching my breath my growing thirst becomes unbearable and I peel my sweaty jeans off and head for the stream.

A long and refreshing drink cheers me up a bit and I decide to take a detour via Snail Rock to collect breakfast. But things get worse. I don't know whether snails can talk to each other, or count, but as I turn over yet another rock to reveal nothing more than a few scurrying sand fleas, it's obvious that there are a lot less snails around than there were yesterday, and at the rate I'm consuming them, what's left will last no more than another day or two at most. I need to ration how many I take and I need to find another food source.

As I replace the heavy rock I trap my finger tip beneath it and cry out, and an echoing cry comes from the river – the otters are back!

It takes no more than a second or two for me to decide that my chores can wait and the best thing for me to do is rest my finger for a while. I head for the bank opposite Otter Rock but as I round the bend I'm amazed to see the mother otter on my side of the river, rummaging amongst the sunken roots of the crooked tree, with her pup close behind her. Tingling with anticipation, I move as close as I dare to the tree and settle down in the shade to watch her.

Breathtaking! So agile. So unbelievably fast. The mother otter doesn't swim so much as flow, weaving in and out of the tangled roots and up and over rocks, probing for fish. And when a big fish breaks cover and makes a dash for deep water, she switches to turbo boost. Like a torpedo locked on its target she reacts to every change of direction with incredible speed and anticipation, twisting and turning, closing the distance between herself and her prey as if joined to the fish by some invisible, unbreakable cord until, no more than thirty seconds after it began, the chase is over. Once targeted, the fish didn't stand a chance, not against the otter. She's the ultimate predator. She is the Amazon.

When I reach camp, the fire is out and it takes a lot of valuable time and effort to relight it. I should have finished the job and put the log on the fire before I took a break and avoided all this hassle. Lesson learned.

As soon as the log is alight I boil the dozen snails I've collected. In the bright light of day their grey flesh looks even less appetising than last night, but I'm famished and eat them anyway, and gulp down the last of the water in my bowl. The snails barely make a dent in my appetite but mentally at least I feel a little better and ready to tackle another chore.

Creating smoke for the rescue signal is easy. All I have to do is dunk armfuls of leafy branches in the river and gently lay them on the fire and thick smoke belches skywards without the fire going out.

I'm more than a little impressed with my efforts and convinced that any plane within miles will be able to see the signal. This cheers me up a bit but my woozy head and aching back tell me I've overdone things again, so I head to the shade of the Joshua Tree to rest and think about my idea.

Hunger pangs wake me sometime in the late afternoon and although I'd told myself I would wait until sunset before eating again, I collect all the remaining snails I can find. I quickly boil and devour half of them, then decide to finish the lot. But even before I've gulped the last one down I start to feel annoyed with myself for my greed and lack of self-control. I've now got nothing to eat tonight.

Thankfully the log is burning even more efficiently than I hoped and with any luck it should last the night, so at least I can put off collecting the other logs until tomorrow.

The sun's position tells me there are a couple of hours of daylight left before dusk, so I place another damp frond on the fire and decide to use the rest of the leafy branches to make a bed.

First I clear sticks and stones from my sleeping area before using one of my shoelaces to tie a bunch of twigs together in a bundle like a witch's broomstick, to sweep the area clean. Then I build a rectangular rock wall about the size of my single bed at home and plug the gaps between the rocks with mud from the stream, hoping to deter the hordes of creepy crawlies.

Next I fill the interior with leafy branches until I have a spongy mattress and after a moment's indecision I fetch my life jacket from the tree and place it at the head of my bed, with the pocket containing Dad's watch on the bottom, cushioned by leaves. By now it's nearly dusk. Time to test my bed. I lie down. No sticks and stones prodding me in the ribs, no hard, uncomfortable lumpy ground, and exactly the right distance from the fire to benefit from the warmth without being bothered by smoke. Result!

With no snails left, I sip my watery but hot snail-flavoured broth. The fire is crackling nicely, with the partially burnt log glowing in the centre, and in the soft light from the fire my bed looks even more impressive. My beautiful handmade bed with its natural stone frame, leafy mattress and air-filled pillow: I grin. I'm proud of myself. I said I'd do something and I did it, without being nagged. Or bribed. Or threatened. Hell, I've even done the equivalent of tidying my room! Mum would be amazed if she could see me now.

But thinking about Mum just reminds me there's no one here to praise me or share in my success and I'm left with a hollow ache instead.

I shake my head and rake the twinkling embers with my stick, releasing a flock of sparks that dance away into the night. Dad doesn't do moping or self-pity, so neither will I. I've survived another day and made progress. Real progress. I've fed myself, improved my situation and increased my chances of being rescued.

And I know what I'll be doing tomorrow. There might even be a tiny part of me that's looking forward to the challenge, even though it's something I've never attempted before. But before yesterday I'd never made fire either.

Tomorrow I'm going to beat the Amazon.

Tomorrow I'm going fishing.

FIFTEEN

It's raining.

My magnificent, life-saving fire has been reduced to nothing more than a mulch of soggy ash and a half-burnt log.

I can't believe I slept through the rain! But then again the Joshua Tree kept most of it off me, and I was so tired, and my new bed was so comfortable. Still is.

My stomach gurgles. I need to eat something. Then I remember there are no snails left, and that's why I have to go fishing. In the rain. And I have to relight the fire.

Now I really want to stay in bed. But I can't. The rain will stop, sooner or later, and I can't bear the thought of another cramp attack. And what if a plane comes and there's no smoke? This last thought is enough to make me get up.

Fortunately the rain has firmed the sand enough for me to be able to roll the remaining two logs back rather than drag them, which requires only a fraction of yesterday's effort, and as I approach the fire with the last log the rain stops and the sun comes out. My mood starts to brighten too.

It will take a while for the wood to dry out enough for me to be able to light the fire so I decide to go fishing while it does.

I don't have a net, or webbed feet and a powerful tail like an otter. But neither does the heron I saw fishing yesterday. He has a beak. So I need a spear.

There is nothing suitable on the ground so I check the low-hanging branches on the nearest trees and choose one from the Joshua Tree, a straight and sturdy branch, about a metre and a half long and a few centimetres thick. Using the sharp edge of my stone hammer I hack at the joint where the branch meets the trunk, trying my best not to cut into the Joshua Tree's trunk. I don't like hurting my tree, my protection and shelter, but the thought of a juicy fish roasting on a spit is enough to keep me hacking away until the branch droops and I can twist it free of the trunk.

Then I try my best to whittle one end to a point. It's a bit off-centre and not exactly sharp, but it will have to do.

With my jeans and socks draped over branches to dry, I pull my pants and damp T-shirt back on and jog barefoot to the spot where I saw the heron fishing yesterday, opposite Otter Rock.

No heron. Good. No competition.

No otters. Also good. For once. I don't have to worry about scaring them away.

I step into the water and shuffle through the shallows, feeling the mud squelch between my toes and trying not to think about what might be hiding in it. When the water laps the bottom of my knees I halt and lean forward, back to the sun, and hold my spear a few centimetres above the surface. I wait for the mud to settle, eagerly scanning for fish. A shoal of inquisitive minnows move in to investigate my legs – an excellent sign! Where there are small fish there should be big fish too. I grip my spear a little tighter and wait for the big ones to arrive.

Hours later all I have to show for my patience are stinging eyes, a raging thirst, and the sour taste of failure.

It shouldn't be this hard!

I know the river is full of fish, the heron and the otters showed me that. So where the hell are they?

The back of my neck is seriously sunburnt and my skull feels like it's being baked in an oven. I'm about to give up and head for the stream when a dark cylindrical shape, about the length of my foot, cruises into view and hovers above the riverbed a few metres away, well within range.

Aches and pains forgotten, my entire focus transfers to the fish, and as steadily as I can I raise my spear and adjust my balance, but my slight movements send a tremor through the water and as I draw my arm back the fish curls left, and with a lazy sweep of his tail he is gone. I stare in disbelief at the puff of mud marking his departure.

My legs are shaking and anger boils in my head. I am about to scream in frustration when the fish returns to the same spot, with his head facing away from me. Perfect.

This time my balance is good and my feet are already in position, with no further adjustments required, so there should be no risk of alerting the fish to my presence. I pull my arm back.

And as I do so the shadow cast by my tilting forearm touches the fish's tail. Then skims along his body and into his eyes. I see his tail fin tense and I know that in a millisecond he will flee. And even though I know it's already too late, I launch my spear, and the point pierces the puff of silt left behind by the fish's thrashing tail, an arm's length away from where he appeared to be.

I grab clumps of my frizzled hair and stamp my feet and scream, then fall backwards into the water, thrashing my arms and kicking my legs like a toddler.

All that food gone. All that time wasted!

My spear floats by and I grab it and stand, and with it grasped tightly in both hands, I lift it to snap it in two across my knee. A tiny spark of common sense registers how thick and strong the shaft is and tells my steaming mind that the stick is more likely to break my kneecap than the other way around. So I fling it at the shoreline instead, and miss the dark spot I was aiming for by some distance. Who am I trying to kid? The stick is no spear, and I'm no heron.

I lie in the shallows for a while, peeling water-softened scabs off my arms until the water cools my neck and head, and I can ignore my thirst no longer.

After a bellyful of stream water I trudge back to the river to retrieve my stick. As I bend to pick it up I can see the second dark shape I was aiming at is the bloated remains of a catfish. A minging, disgusting dead lump of green flesh, crawling with maggots.

Hand over mouth I turn to leave, and my attention is caught by a shoal of minnows darting to and fro in the shallows, glinting like scraps of tinfoil in the sun. They seem to be fighting over something – my scabs. I grunt in disgust. Where are the big fish, the ones the heron and the otters catch? The ones worth eating. Then, without being consciously aware I'm doing it, I start to count the minnows. I stop at thirty.

And this time I don't see tiddlers or scraps of tinfoil. I see food. I've eaten small fish before – whitebait, admittedly only once, and the fact that they still had their heads on freaked me out, and I could only stomach them when they were smothered in mayonnaise, but that doesn't seem important now. Food is food, fish is fish, and half a dozen minnows would make a decent mouthful.

But my stick's no good and I have no net, so how can I catch them? I sit on the bank and roll a scab between my thumb and forefinger, and I have an idea.

Water laps my bottom. My knees are bent to ninety degrees and my cupped hands are resting on the riverbed, knuckles down and fingers spread wide, with a scab from my arm rocking in the centre. After a few long minutes a minnow circles my finger trap, swimming closer and closer, then veering away a dozen times, until it plucks up the courage to dart in and nibble at the bait. My muscles tense and it takes all my willpower not to snap my fingers shut and yank my hands up out of the water, but I know I must be patient, and wait until more fish have entered the trap. Moments later the minnow is joined by three others and I can hold out no longer. As fast as I can, I clamp my fingers together and lift my closed hands up off the riverbed, feeling the touch of a tiny fin as I do so.

I step onto the shore and crouch, barely able to contain my excitement. Did I get all four or did one manage to escape?

I open my hands.

Empty. Not one fish.

I stare at my hands in confusion, stretching my fingers wide to check the gaps and turning my palms over to inspect the backs.

Then I dig through the damp sand for any sign of the minnows.

Nothing. Not one minnow. Not even a fin.

I don't want to believe it. I can't. Part of me wants to scream and part of me wants to cry but I'm too numb, too disappointed. So I do nothing, just sit on the damp sand with shoulders slumped and head in hands, chewing the inside of my gums. I've failed. Again. I'm done. Drained. I just want to go back to bed and sleep, and dream myself far away from here. But somewhere in my brain a faint but stern voice tells me I can't. Tells me I have to stay on my feet. Tells me that if I crawl into bed now I may never get up again. Tells me I can't give up.

No. Bed is not an option. Not if I want to live.

I know what I must do. I must not give up. Somehow I must find a way to catch these bloody fish.

SIXTEEN

Standing stark naked in the mosquito-defying smoke from the fire, eyes streaming and coughing my guts up, I jump, and slap at my leg as the fire spits another spark into my flesh. I flick the ember from my skin and spread my palms wide once more, shielding my bare bottom, and blink through streaming eyes at the blurred shapes lying on the ground before me – every possession I own. It's pitiful. A pile of junk.

But somehow I need to turn this junk into something useful. I need to turn it into something to catch fish.

Another spark, this time embedding itself in my bum cheek. This is ridiculous! I've had enough. I move away from the fire, grab my pants and pull them back on. I leave my socks by the fire to dry. I'd thought about filling one with sand and using it to club fish with, but I doubt I could get close enough to a fish to use it, and anyway, there are holes in both socks and the sand would simply pour out. I have no net and I'm crap with a spear. And I'm no otter. The only idea that makes any sense is the simplest one. To catch a fish I need to be a fisherman.

So to be a fisherman I need a fishing rod, line, hook and bait.

I can use my so-called spear as a rod and my shoelaces tied together will do for the line. It means my trainers will be really loose or I'll have to go barefoot from now on but I figure it's worth it. Now all I need is a hook and some bait.

I pick up Dad's watch. After much agonising I prise the dial off but to my dismay I can't find anything to use as a hook. Until I notice the wire pin connecting the strap to the body, and after some painful biting and twisting I manage to break it free. It's far from ideal but it will have to do.

Now all I need is some bait.

And I know just where to get it.

In less than twenty-four hours the catfish has been reduced to a shrivelled sausage of skin littered with tiny brown cigar-shaped pupae. I flick what's left of it over with my stick to reveal half a dozen maggots, and scrape all six into my bowl before quickly walking across to the spot on the riverbank where the minnows evaded me yesterday. Pinching a maggot from the bowl I try to impale it on my hook without dropping it or pricking my thumb.

The maggot squirms from my grip and falls to the sand and I swear, and wipe my hands on my T-shirt while I try to calm down and tell myself to be more patient. Squeezing the writhing grub more firmly this time, I hook the wire into a crease in the maggot's taut body, and steadily increase the pressure until with a sudden give the point pierces the skin.

The maggot thrashes violently on the hook and I quickly extend my rod over the bank and drop my bait in the water. I watch in excited anticipation as it sinks, twitching. Within seconds the minnows appear and go straight for the bait. As one swallows it I yank my rod up and can hardly believe my eyes when I see the small silver fish dangling from the end.

I pull my rod in and grab the minnow. After a moment's hesitation I tap its head hard against the rod and cram it into my mouth. It seems to be more bones than flesh and tastes extremely salty, like an anchovy, and I hate anchovies. But it's food, and I'm too famished to care. In two swallows it's gone and the maggot is still whole and wriggling so I drop it back into the water, a huge grin spreading across my face.

For every fish I land I lose two or three more, some of which are injured and ripped apart by the rest of the shoal, but in no time at all I have caught and consumed five minnows, and another eight lie on the sand next to me. I reach into my bowl to bait the hook again and pause. I only have one maggot left. I should quit now, cook the fish I've caught and save the remaining grub for later. But there are more minnows than ever, and for the first time in ages I'm enjoying myself. So I bait my hook with the last maggot and cast.

The grub sinks. A minnow grabs it. And in that instant, that nanosecond before I strike, the minnow is engulfed in a snare of jagged teeth. The line goes taut, the rod's tip bends towards the water and the minnow disappears in a swirl of flashing red and silver scales, along with my hook and a length of shoelace.

My fishing is over. Hook gone. But even the loss of the precious hook can't dent my feelings of success and satisfaction. My contraption worked. It actually worked! I have a decent haul of minnows to cook and I can use the other pin on Dad's watch strap to make another hook. There was something thrilling about the piranha's attack and in the back of my mind an idea is starting to form.

The fire is still smouldering when I reach camp and I hurriedly add more wood and place my bowl of fresh water on the rock to boil. None of the minnows are more than a few centimetres long, far too small to try to gut, so I drop four into the water whole and keep the other four for later, wrapped in a leaf and tucked in my sock for safekeeping.

After a few minutes the heat softens the fishes' bones and the opaque flesh turns white and breaks apart. I lift the bowl, blow, and sip. OK, so my fish soup isn't exactly delicious but diluted by stream water, the minnows' saltiness works in my favour, seasoning the broth. At least it's better than snail soup and I'm more than a little impressed with my cooking skills and self-control, especially when I make four small fish stretch over three big bowls of broth.

The fish soup provides a much needed boost to both my body and my determination, and I spend the rest of the day cleaning camp, tending to the smoke signal, and hauling logs. By sunset the camp is neat and tidy, my bed has a fresh leafy mattress and I have at least three days' worth of logs piled up which, with any luck, I won't have to use.

It's time to turn my attention to my big idea.

'Use a sprat to catch a mackerel!'

That's what Gran used to say and that's exactly what I intend to do. I don't know if I can make this work but I'm certainly going to try. And I do know one thing for sure.

I'm going to need a bigger hook.

SEVENTEEN

Wide awake and too excited to stay fidgeting in bed any longer, I'm up and at the river before dawn, jogging up and down the riverbank and rubbing my arms in the pre-dawn chill.

As the sun's soft glow lights the horizon I stand completely still and stare, amazed by the way the spreading sunlight colours the trees and melts the fog blanketing the river, and I realise that I've never made the effort to watch a sunrise before. It's spectacular.

A few minutes later I reckon it's light enough for me to give it a try. I unwind the shoelaces from the shaft of my new pole, twice the thickness of my previous one, and catch hold of my new piranha-proof hook, made from the reinforcing wire of the life jacket. My fingers still ache from the hours of twisting and tearing it took to extract it, but by taking my time and carefully unpicking the seams I managed to get the wire out in one piece, without puncturing the jacket's air chambers. Pretty soon I'll know if it was worth it.

Time to fish! I hook a minnow through its glazed eye and drop it in the water, hands trembling with excitement. There is no wind and the water is so still I can clearly see the circles rippling out from where the quivering wire enters the water. Fixing my eyes on the minnow I wait for the piranhas to arrive.

An hour or two later the sun is a hell of a lot hotter and much higher in the sky, and the only thing that's feeding is the mosquitoes. On me.

I don't get it! I'm in exactly the same spot as I was yesterday, so what was different then? What made the piranhas come? I slap at a mosquito chewing on my arm and stare at the smudge of blood left behind.

Blood! That's why the piranhas came. They must have tasted the blood and fluids from the maggots and crippled minnows. If I want to attract piranhas then I need to send a message; a bloody 'Breakfast is served' broadcast to get their attention.

But I only have two minnows left and the last maggot turned into a chrysalis overnight. No problem. I'll use my own blood instead.

I peel a freshly formed scab off my arm, clamp my mouth over the wound, suck up the blood, and spit the scab and blood into the water. As the scab sinks I quickly drop my minnow in the centre of the bloody cloud and jig it up and down, to mimic an injured fish, but I don't jig too hard – I don't want the minnow to disintegrate. More blood is seeping from my arm and dripping onto the sand so I suck up another mouthful and spit that in as well.

Two gobs. Thirty seconds. That's all it takes.

Less than a teaspoon of blood is enough to summon a shoal of voracious piranhas from every direction, churning the water, zeroing in on the bait.

Wow they're quick! Lightning fast. The first piranha to arrive rips the minnow from my hook and vanishes before I can even think about striking. I yell, and thump the ground in frustration.

I was too sluggish to react in time. Far too slow. I rub my palms together hard and fast and slap my face. I'm going to have to be much quicker than that.

I hook my last minnow and drop it in the water. This time I'm fully tensed and alert and as soon as a piranha seizes the bait I strike in a swift upward motion that wrenches the fish from the water. Swinging the rod around as quickly as I can, I drop the fish on the ground above the riverbank. The piranha hits the earth with a thud, the impact dislodges the hook from its mouth and in two tail-flexing springs it bounces off the bank and into the river. I scream, '*No!*' and scrabble to the edge of the bank and peer into the water, but it's no good, the fish has gone.

That was my last minnow. I pick up my hook. Half the minnow is left, enough for one last cast. Focus!

This time, the instant the minnow hits the water and I feel a tug on the line I strike, and hook the piranha securely through its jaw. I swing it onto the bank, and as it meets the ground I grab my rock and scramble across to it, and slam the rock down on the piranha's head over and over again, bashing it as hard as I can until its eye pops from its socket and its jaw breaks. I'm panting, heart racing, and my T-shirt is splattered in blood and scales.

I stick two fingers into the piranha's mouth to retrieve my hook but as I do so the fish bucks and its teeth graze across my knuckles, slicing the skin. Man those teeth are sharp! With its head smashed to a bloody pulp the fish is clearly dead and that was no more than a muscle reflex action, but I bash its head in again anyway, purely out of spite, then suck up the blood pouring from my throbbing knuckle and spit it into the water.

I have no minnows left but it doesn't matter. The piranhas are in no hurry to leave and this fish will provide me with all the bait I need. I take great pleasure in pulverising the piranhas to a pile of bait-sized pieces and chucking the bloody remains back in the water, to keep its cannibalistic mates around.

A dozen casts later, seven piranhas lie on the ground beside me. Seven fish! More than enough. More than I could have dared hope for. A feast!

But the fish are not only a feast for me. Swarms of biting black flies have arrived and it's only a matter of time before the ants appear, and I'm covered in minging fish blood and guts. Time to go.

With the fish wrapped in my T-shirt and my rod balanced on my shoulder, I hurry back to camp, licking my cracked lips at the thought of the feast ahead. I've done well. Really well. If only someone could see me now!

I stop. Keen as I am to cook and eat my catch there's somewhere I want to go first.

Yes! The otters are on their rock, mother pinning the pup down and licking his head while he squeaks in complaint and tries to wriggle free.

I place my T-shirt on the ground, select the two biggest

fish and lift them high in the air, jerking them up and down to get the mother's attention. I so want her to see me, to see what I've done. Almost immediately my boastful display catches her eye and she pauses in cleaning her pup to peer in my direction, and thankfully this time she doesn't tense or get ready to flee. Instead she sniffs the breeze and adjusts her stance to get a better view. Then she relaxes and grunts, and I choose to believe it's a grunt of approval. I choose to believe she's impressed.

The pup takes advantage of the break in Mum's attention to wriggle out from under her and escape into the river. Mum watches him go, then yawns and starts grooming herself.

Watching the mother clean herself I become aware of how grimy and sweaty I am, and how much I reek of fish blood and guts. I could really do with a good wash too. But as appealing as the river appears, I'm not going in. Not after what I've just seen. Not covered in smelly fish guts and with my knuckle still seeping blood. I'm still stunned by the effect just a few drops of blood can have on piranhas and I try not to think of the many times I sat in the river scratching bloody scabs off my skin.

But my sticky hands really are too disgusting to put up with any longer and I can at least wash the blood and scales from them without having to enter the river.

I walk to the water's edge and dip my hands in. I'm concentrating on prising a sharp fish scale out from under my thumbnail when there's a sudden disturbance on the surface a few metres away. I jump and jerk my hands from the water so quickly I lose my balance and tumble backwards.

But to my relief it's not a piranha. Or a caiman. It's the otter pup!

He bobs, and paddles closer, so close I can clearly see his teddy bear nose, glinting liquid-brown eyes and ruff of magnificent whiskers. He's beautiful. Ridiculously cute. Holding his head clear of the surface like a periscope the pup treads water, and it's apparent by his chirping and the way his nostrils flare and his whiskers twitch that he's bursting with curiosity, desperate to see what's wrapped in my T-shirt. He's also completely unafraid, and I realise I'm probably the first human he's ever seen.

I purse my lips to whistle hello, but all that comes out is a deflated raspberry followed by a wheeze and a cough, and the pup huffs then makes a farting noise in response. Another sound swiftly follows and for a moment I wonder what the strange noise is, and where it has come from, and then I realise it is laughter, and it has come from me. It's been a long time.

I clear my throat and try again. 'Come on, Pup,' I say, as encouragingly as I can. 'Come and have a look.'

The pup chitters and moves a little closer to the bank. Then he glances back across the river at Mum, dozing in the sun. I can tell he's torn between his desire to see what's hidden in my T-shirt and concern that Mum will see him and tell him off for straying too far again.

He chirps once more, this time with a hint of frustration, and Mum wakes and calls him back with a sharp two-tone whistle. I don't want him to go but I don't want him to get in trouble either. I look down at my fish, my precious piranhas, and throw him one. It's a poor throw and the fish lands with a splash a couple of metres to the pup's left and he disappears. For a moment I'm worried I've screwed up and scared him away but then his head breaks surface, with my piranha held firmly in his jaws. With a flick of his tail he kicks hard and swims back towards Mum.

I watch the pup porpoise away, his paddle tail pumping and my fish glinting in his mouth, and I'm thrilled, beaming with delight, and as the pup clambers onto the rock and dodges a cuff from Mum, I have an irresistible urge to give him a name. I can't keep calling him Pup. Not now we've actually met. I look at the way his wet fur gleams in the sun, smooth and silky and chocolate brown, and I think about the way I'm feeling right at this moment. And I know what to call him. I'll name him after my favourite chocolate. The smoothest, tastiest chocolate in the world. I'll call him Galaxy.

PART TWO

EIGHTEEN

Just the one fish for breakfast. Perhaps two...

For three days I've been pigging out on piranhas. Spit-roasted or fried on hot rocks for breakfast. Cold for lunch. Best of all; slow oven-baked for dinner, and with each meal I can feel my strength returning.

I select two medium-sized fish, lay them flat on the rock and scrape the scales off with my piranha knife, version five, made from the rigid jaw bone and serrated teeth of the biggest piranha I've caught so far, and bound to a stick handle with life-jacket wire. It's wickedly sharp. Well worth all the skin and blood it cost to make it!

After descaling, gutting and rinsing the fish I wrap them in vine leaves, dip the package in the stream and jog back to camp, pausing on the way to lay the knife at the foot of the ant tree, to be picked clean before nightfall.

The parcel is still nicely damp when I reach camp and place it in the oven I've constructed beneath the fire: a stone-walled pit with a rock trapdoor for access. Wrapped in the wet leaves and shielded from the full force of the fire, the fish will bake slowly during the day and this evening the flesh will still be moist and will literally fall off the bone – delicious! Even better than Dad's jacket potatoes I reckon, and I like to think he'd be impressed.

Breakfast over, I return to the stream to bathe and clean my teeth, using my moss sponge to wash my face and armpits, and handfuls of sand to shift the more engrained filth and fish guts from my hands and arms. Shredded twigs do a pretty good job as a toothbrush, dislodging the fish bones which get stuck between my teeth. I just wish I had some toothpaste to shift the fur coating them, and to sort out my minging breath...

With the protein boost from the fish and my new daily hygiene ritual kicking in, bites and scratches heal more quickly and don't itch for as long. My skin is a colour it's never been before and the soles of my feet are like tough leather and don't burn on the hot sand any more. I'm sleeping better at night as well and no longer wake at the slightest disturbance or take much notice of the screeching birds and monkeys. And my camp site is getting better by the day.

My days are my own and I decide what to do with them, and when. I decide when to go to bed and when to get up. When to start my chores and how much time to spend on each one. And with no watch, clock or phone to refer to, it's as if what I used to know as time has no meaning now. Not hours or minutes anyway. Daylight yes, and night-time. But I no longer think in terms of hours and minutes passed, or hours still to come, instead I simply measure the passage of each day in terms of tasks done, or yet to do.

Back in camp I stretch and yawn, a long and satisfying one. I fight the urge to lie down on my new bed, with its layer of soft leafy branches resting on a base of thicker ones, to keep me off the damp, lumpy ground and clear of the creepy crawlies.

No. I'll stick to my routine. I'll clean the camp site first, fetch wood, and stoke the fire. Then it will be time for my midday nap. This afternoon I'll check the *HELP* sign and forage along the shoreline for food before settling down to watch the otters fish and play through sunset. 'Otter Time' is something I really look forward to, an incentive to get things done, and it's my favourite part of the day.

When the otters have gone I'll sit with my back resting against the Joshua Tree, reflect on the day, and make plans for the next one.

It's an entirely new experience for me; just sitting and thinking, with no external stimulation or distractions. Before now the idea would have horrified me. Now I see it as a well-earned reward and a chance to rest and replay the day, and think of more ways to improve my situation. And it's time well spent, even if not every idea works. The sad excuse for a sun hat I tried to plait out of palm leaves and the piranha-teeth comb that just snagged in my knotted hair prove that.

But Dad says that we learn from every failure and I want to believe he's right as I pick up the orange-sized seed pod and press a paste of stream mud and chewed up grass stems into the last crack I can find. If I've finally got the paste's consistency right and I've found every crack in the husk, then I might just turn this pod – number nine – into a drinking cup after all.

After a final inspection I wrap one of my socks around the base for comfort and reach for my cooking pot, filled with water, and try not to think about the eight failures I've flung into the river since yesterday. Dad would say they were 'prototypes', not failures.

But if this doesn't work that's it. I'm done. I'm out of pods, paste and patience.

I slowly pour water into the pod, a little at a time, then sit back and stare, expecting to see the familiar stain spread across the rock at any moment. Seconds pass. No stain. I check the water level. It hasn't dropped. I pick the pod up. The sock isn't wet. Not even damp. It works!

'Dad, look, I've done it!'

I'm off my feet and spinning around, sploshing water on myself, before I'm even aware the words have left my mouth.

Silence.

No 'Let me see'. No 'Hooray!' No high fives. No hug. I take two deep breaths, splat a fly lapping the water from my skin and stare at the thing in my hand.

My great invention. My triumph. It's leaking.

NINETEEN

No piranhas. I've been fishing for an hour or more with no luck, not even a nibble. For once the fish aren't interested. Perhaps the otters have spooked them, or they've sussed me, or found something tastier elsewhere.

Slumped and sulking in the shrinking shade of the crooked tree I'm half-heartedly trying to summon up the energy to return to camp and get on with my chores before the heat cranks up.

But I'm hungry, I've had nothing to eat for breakfast and I really don't like this break in my routine. And the sight of Galaxy tucking into his fourth crab of the morning certainly isn't improving my mood. Tongue slapping sounds and grunts of satisfaction tell me how much he's enjoying it, and I'm envious as hell. I like crab, the white meat anyway. Admittedly I've only had it once but I can still remember the delicate taste and the firm but juicy texture of the curved chunk of claw meat, tinged with pink, drizzled with lemon juice and dipped in melted butter. OK so the small green crabs Galaxy is dismembering look nothing like the brick-red one I had, and would probably give me cramps and raging diarrhoea, but that's not the point. My stomach is grumbling and I've given Galaxy loads of fish, so where's my crab!

It must be another ten minutes or so before the sun starts to grill the tops of my feet, forcing me to move. Only then, as I stand and turn to leave, do I stop feeling sorry for myself long enough to notice that Galaxy's mum has been away for much longer than usual. She's never let Galaxy out of her sight for more than a few minutes before, and never when he's been on my side of the river. So instead of heading directly back to camp I walk to the river's edge and scan the water for any sign of her. Meanwhile, Galaxy continues playing with his empty crab shell, flicking it high in the air with his tail and catching it before it hits the water, seemingly unaware of his mother's absence.

Another minute or two passes with no sign of Galaxy's mum and I'm starting to get seriously concerned. Even Galaxy seems to sense something is wrong. He drops the crab shell, clambers up the riverbank and stands on his hind legs, chirping and whistling, with a shrill note of anxiety in his voice. I move further along the bank to get a better view upstream, squinting hard as I look directly into the sun, and as I do so the mother otter appears below me and to my right, her head breaking water between Galaxy and me.

She pauses at the water's edge before slowly emerging, head bowed and moving with some difficulty, and at first I think she must have injured herself. But then I see the reason for her unsteadiness. Slung between her legs is the biggest catfish I have ever seen, as thick as my arm and as long as the otter. Its eel-like black body writhes and coils, as if the fish is trying to wrap itself around its captor, but even from this distance I can clearly see the fish's head swinging like a pendulum from the gaping V-shaped wound where the otter has bitten through its neck, nearly decapitating it.

Galaxy spins round at the sound of his mother's return and gallops down the bank to greet her, squeaking with delight. He licks her face, then grabs the catfish as she releases it and climbs a couple of metres higher to the grassy verge before slumping down, panting. Galaxy lets her go, his full attention now on the catfish as he pounces on its coils and bites its neck.

The mother otter remains flat out for a minute or two before painstakingly washing herself, licking the insides of her paws a dozen times then drawing them across her cheeks and whiskers to clean catfish slime from her face.

Relieved she's not injured, and only half-realising she's never been this close to me before, I turn my attention to Galaxy just in time to see him bite clean through the catfish's neck, and I clap and cheer, and as I do so I suddenly have the strangest feeling I'm being studied, scrutinized. I turn my head. The mother otter is looking directly at me, staring piercingly into my eyes, and as I hold her stare I could swear she gives the briefest nod of her head before stretching out and closing her eyes.

That evening, after a meagre supper of a few fish scraps washed down with hot water, I replay what happened at the riverbank. Yes, I was tired and grumpy, and my eyes were still watering from the sun's glare when the mother otter's eyes met mine, and it's more than likely that I imagined the nod. But the more times I rewind and play the moment, the more I can't help thinking that, extraordinary as it seems, maybe, just maybe, the mother otter left Galaxy in my care deliberately, and

I have been tried and tested, and I have passed. I like the thought.

After this the mother otter's attitude towards me changes. She no longer summons Galaxy back if he swims to my side of the river, and she leaves him with me more often when she heads off to hunt on her own, seemingly having given up trying to teach Galaxy how to hunt. Despite her best efforts, Galaxy continues to display no interest whatsoever in catching his own fish. Eating them, yes. Hunting them, no. He'd much rather play, and I'd much rather watch him than work.

Galaxy finds everything fascinating, no matter how simple. A round pebble can keep him amused for hours as he juggles it, or rolls it up and down his belly. Not surprisingly he's particularly thrilled by anything that floats – sticks, leaves, and an occasional unfortunate beetle. And empty crab shells become attacking enemy boats to be patted back across the surface, or sunk with a well-aimed blow.

Flittering butterflies enchant and frustrate him in equal measure, and he regularly knackers himself out leaping high to try to catch one. When on land his slinky tail becomes a fleeing eel to be pursued at lightning speed as he spins round and round as fast as he can, until dizziness overcomes him and he falls over and pants. Then when he's worn out and there's no Mum around to snuggle up to, he loves to float on his back in the calm waters beneath the overhanging branches of the crooked tree, tail curled around a root and paws gently flexing on his chest, gazing wide-eyed at the leaves dancing in the dappled sunlight above and cooing like a baby entranced by a twirling mobile.

These magical hours spent with Galaxy race by, especially once I convince myself I'm keeping an eye on him out of a sense of parental responsibility rather than laziness.

While foraging for nuts one afternoon I'm delighted to find a hollow seed pod, as big as a tennis ball. It's possibly light enough to float and, best of all, when I shake the pod it rattles! I cut short my search and jog back to camp. I can't wait to give it to Galaxy.

Galaxy's dozing, sprawled in the shade of the crooked tree, head on paws and tail in the water, but his eyes open at the sound of my approach and although I'm dying to give him the seed pod straight away, I decide to try something first. I sit down about five metres away from him, legs crossed, arms resting on my knees to hide the pod, and I start to grunt and emit soft whistles of admiration over the unseen object nestled in my lap.

At first Galaxy just snorts and closes his eyes again, but then when I toss the pod in the air and it rattles, his eyes spring open and he's up and on his feet in a flash, bounding towards me. But halfway across he stops and sits back on his haunches, in the full heat of the sun, and starts to fidget and chitter with frustration. He seriously wants the seed pod and I really want to give it to him, but even though I shake it and toss it in the air again he won't come any closer, and I won't let him have it, not just yet.

I shuffle round until my back is to Galaxy and gently rattle the pod again, hoping the loss of eye contact will make me appear less threatening, and his desire and curiosity will be enough to overcome his apprehension. After a few moments Galaxy's chittering becomes a sort of mewing, and it's clear he's getting closer. Quaking with excitement, I rattle the seed pod every few seconds to encourage him and boost his interest. Inch by inch Galaxy shuffles closer, until I can tell by his loud snuffling that he's directly behind me. I fight the urge to turn around and try to stroke him, terrified I'll scare him away.

Keeping my back to him I pretend to be so engrossed in the seed pod I haven't noticed his presence, but he's so close now I can smell him. He smells of fish, and wet fur and... something else, something familiar and refreshing and completely out of place. And while I'm trying to identify the odour I feel a sudden bump on my elbow and a tickling sensation. It's his nose and whiskers. Galaxy's touched me! The sudden shock is electric and it takes all my willpower not to cry out and spin round. Instead I slowly raise my trembling hand and extend it to him, like Dad taught me to do with dogs, so Galaxy can sniff me, and know I pose no threat.

The feel of Galaxy's warm breath and then the caress of his wet tongue on my fingers send a shiver through my body and it's all I can do not to grab him and give him a hug. I somehow steady myself, swallow the lump in my throat, and give him the seed pod instead.

And as Galaxy bounds away with his new toy rattling in his mouth, he leaves a lingering scent behind. I inhale it, and I know what else he smells of besides fish and wet fur. He smells of freshly mown grass. He smells of good times. He smells of home.

TWENTY

Over the next few days, by focusing on the task in hand and resisting all distractions, I complete my chores in record time to free up more of each day to spend with the otters. Without being aware of having made a conscious decision to do so, I've started talking to Galaxy. Just brief comments to begin with, taking the mickey mostly, or giving him a hard time for being so lazy. But now I tell him all about what I've been up to since I saw him last, how many fish I've caught, how many ticks and mosquitoes I've slain, and my latest innovation.

What at first felt a bit stupid feels perfectly natural now, and I look forward to our conversations, even if they are a bit one-sided. And now I've got myself a healthy stockpile of firewood, discovered some nuts to supplement my fish diet, and run out of ideas of how to improve the camp site, I've decided to do something about the language barrier. I've decided to learn how to talk otter.

To my surprise, I willingly put more effort into understanding how the otters communicate than I ever did in any foreign language lesson at school. The otters talk so fast it's all a jumble to begin with and I come close to giving up a number of times. But by narrowing my focus to only one specific note or expression at a time, I start to identify and separate the diverse range of sounds and gestures they use to communicate and express emotions – the burring squeak and nose-kiss for greeting. The grunts and chirps for happiness. Snuffles and hugs for affection. The differently toned huffs and pants for laughter, or irritation. Chittering for curiosity. Barks for frustration. Shrill squeals and whines for anger. Teeth-baring howls for warning. Purrs, sighs and belly rubs for contentment.

With each success, every subsequent study session becomes more complex, more challenging, and each breakthrough more rewarding. It's an eye-opening experience for me.

I had no idea I could be so disciplined. So patient. Setting my own targets and sticking to them for however long it takes, without being told to or supervised, and with no promise of reward or risk of punishment. No instructions. No feedback. No feeling I'm missing out on something else. I had no idea I could concentrate on one thing for so long, staying so calm and focused that my mind settles, my surroundings disappear, and time neither crawls nor flies, it just passes.

My early efforts are atrocious and I'm convinced my mouth and tongue must be the wrong shape to form the sounds correctly. But then a few noises start to sound about right, and by day three I'm mimicking the otters' calls. Only when they're not around, and only the simpler one-note grunts and clicks to begin with. And now I'm happy I've mastered those I decide it's time to tackle the hardest call of all – the mother otter's crisp two-tone *To me!* whistle.

The woodpile dwindles to a few logs and branches, my bedding remains unchanged, clothes unwashed, and I even deny myself the pleasure of Galaxy's company while I sit beneath the Joshua Tree and try to replicate the *To me!* call. I scream and sulk in equal measure, grind my furry teeth and thump the Joshua Tree in frustration until eventually, late in the afternoon, after many hundreds of repetitions, a two-tone *To me!* whistling sound exits my cracked and bleeding lips, and with a huge sense of relief I think I may have got it.

But I'm too drained to celebrate and the truth is I won't

know if I've nailed the call until I give it a try, and that will have to wait until this evening, after I've changed my bedding, and had a lie-down, and given my lips a break.

The air is chilly. Squadrons of yapping fruit bats are heading across the river to feed while flocks of rowdy parrots stream home to roost. Galaxy and his mum are heading home too, and already halfway across the river by the time I summon up the courage to give the *To me!* call a try. I clear my throat, purse my lips and whistle, two crisp tones, one after the other, hoping Galaxy can hear me above the bats and birds.

Galaxy stops midstream, spins round and starts to swim towards me, and only when his mother counters my call with one of her own does he pause, twirling around in confusion. Beside myself with excitement I whistle again, and Galaxy starts swimming towards me again before Mum calls him back, more firmly this time, and I clamp my hands over my mouth and keep my lips clenched shut until the otters have swum out of view. Only then do I leap to my feet and punch the air and whistle *To me! To me!* over and over again. I've done it. I've done it! The sense of accomplishment is as exhilarating as when I created fire, and caught my first piranha. I've done it again. I've achieved the impossible. I can talk otter.

TWENTY-ONE

Midday and it's raining. Again.

I'm stripped down to my pants but still sweating buckets as I haul a heavy branch through the thick foliage. Having used up all the driftwood along the sandspit, and unwilling to enter the jungle, I now have to fetch wood from much further along the riverbank and today I'm a long way from camp, out of sight around a steep-sided bend. And with less time to fish or harvest nuts and fruit, the constant gnawing hunger has returned. But I can handle it. I'm leaner and stronger than I've ever been and I reckon my stomach must have shrunk to less than half its previous size. And following my worrying discovery of big paw prints in the mud by the stream it didn't take long for me to decide to prioritise the fire over food. But then a loud rumble in my stomach reminds me I haven't eaten all day, so I decide to take a break and check around for nuts and fruit.

The first few trees I check are bare so I walk further along the bank. While scanning the next tree I notice a cavity in the trunk of the dead tree beside it, three or four metres off the ground, with twigs and straw sticking out, possibly a bird's nest. With eggs!

The dead tree is branchless apart from a few stumps above the cavity and the trunk is too smooth to get a grip, but by climbing the branches of the neighbouring tree I am able to lean across and reach it. Steadying myself against the trunk I whisper, 'Please let there be eggs, please let there be eggs,' and peer inside, preparing myself for the exit of a startled bird. But instead of a brooding bird or a clutch of eggs, curled within the moss-lined chamber is the most beautiful creature I have ever seen. A ball of glinting golden fur, about the size of a squirrel, with a long bushy tail wrapped around its face and waves of shimmering gold rippling down its body as its tiny chest rises and falls. I freeze, hunger forgotten as I watch this gorgeous animal sleep. I instantly recognise it from the photos Gran kept in her bedside drawer, the ones she cut out of *National Geographic* magazine, but I can still hardly believe my eyes. Hardly believe that I'm looking at a golden lion tamarin, one of the rarest and most endangered creatures on earth and the one animal Gran wanted to see above all others!

I hold my breath as the tamarin stretches its paws, cat-like, and turns its head just enough for me to get a peek at its magnificent mane of bushy golden fur, and a soft 'Wow!' escapes my lips. Thankfully the tamarin doesn't wake. I so want to stroke it, but I won't risk alarming it, so I take one last look then climb back down the tree as quietly as I can.

Brushing twigs and minute red spiders from my sticky skin, I gaze up at the hole in the dead tree's trunk to reassure myself I'm not dreaming. A golden lion tamarin! Man, how I wish Gran was here.

Walking a little further along the riverbank, I'm about to start checking a clump of promising-looking trees, with foliage similar to the papaya tree by the ravine, when I hear something else besides the droning insects and tapping rain. It sounds like the mother otter's bark, and I can hear Galaxy's distinctive squeaks too! Eager to see them I push through tall bushes to the top of the riverbank. A landslide has swept most of the vegetation from this section of the bank, creating a wide tree-free gap all the way down to the river below. I lean out and peer down, and see Galaxy racing diagonally up the slope, and looking across to where he's heading, I can see the reason for his haste. Chiselled into the bank is a mud slide, carved by a fallen tree – a steep chute of slick, glossy mud fed by a small stream and ending in a waterfall with a drop of a couple of metres to the river's surface below.

I'm still staring at the waterfall when Galaxy leaps into the top of the slide, toboggans down at great speed and shoots out into mid-air in a whirling tangle of limbs and tail before plummeting into the water with a cry of pure glee.

'Wow!' I yell, and start clapping. The mother otter jumps in alarm and dives into the water. But I barely notice. My attention is on Galaxy, and the fun he's having, and although the nagging part of my brain tells me this is a really bad idea, and I could easily injure myself, I'm too hot and excited to be sensible. I'm having a go!

Hurrying across to the top of the slide, I'm about to jump into the wet chute when some lingering scrap of common sense tells me not to risk losing my pants, so I quickly take them off and hang them on the nearest bush.

Swimming far below, Galaxy looks up at me and barks, as if inviting me to join in the fun. I bark back, jump into the chute and careen down the fur-polished slide at breath-snatching speed before cartwheeling through the air with a scream of half elation and half terror. I crash into the water with a huge splash, creating a mini tidal wave that submerges Galaxy and slams against the bank. The water is shockingly cold on my hot skin, and I take a moment to catch my breath, but sliding down that bank is the fastest my body has moved in a long time and the sudden rush of adrenaline is intoxicating. Pumped up and hollering, 'Woo hoo!' at the top of my voice, I'm eager to do it again.

As I start to swim towards the bank Galaxy appears alongside me and yelps, as if challenging me to a race. I yell, 'You're on!' I splash him, and try to front crawl, forgetting I can't. I've never been able to get the breathing right, so I lunge past him and frantically breaststroke instead, as fast as I can, with no style whatsoever and kicking like a disjointed frog. But even with my much longer limbs and a two stroke head start, Galaxy destroys me, and before I've covered even half the distance he's perched high on the log jam at the base of the bank, chattering away to his mum, bombarding her with squeaks and chirps, as if to say,

Did you see what I did, Mum? Did you see what I did? But Mum seems preoccupied and uneasy, staring up the bank and scanning the sky, and with an impatient snicker and teeth clash she shoos Galaxy away. She should lighten up and have a go!

Panting as though laughing, Galaxy stares at me as I emerge from the river, wet hair plastered to my head and water cascading from my goose-bumped skin. He starts to chitter and whistle, no doubt telling me how bad a swimmer I am, and he's right, but I don't care. I blow a loud raspberry in response, figuring it means the same thing in any language, even otter talk, before scrambling up the bank and whooshing down the slide again, tanked up and yelling my head off.

We take it in turns, sort of, with Galaxy completing three or four descents to every one of mine. With every madcap plunge the slide gets slicker and faster and the mud gets everywhere, in my mouth, eyes and ears, up my nose and bum, and I couldn't care less. I even go head first and create the loudest splash and biggest wave yet with an epic bellyflop. 'Yes!' I yell. Galaxy may have the style but I've got the bulk.

And for the next hour or two there is nothing but fun. Nothing but the moment. No rules. No restrictions. No embarrassment about being naked. For an hour or two

I forget where I am. For an hour or two I shout, scream, laugh, get plastered in mud and swallow bucketfuls of water, and I'm as happy as I have ever been. For an hour or two I'm a kid again. No. Better than that. For an hour or two I am an otter.

All too soon Galaxy's mum barks *Time's up!* and calls him to her. She's still tense and fidgety, and seems keen to leave, but Galaxy's knackered anyway, as am I, and I'm not too disappointed when they disappear around the bend.

I'm alone, cold in my nakedness, and covered in bruises. But I'm also refreshed and buzzing, and ready to have a go at hauling the branch back to camp. I climb back up the bank and walk to the bush I hung my pants on. They've fallen to the bottom. I reach through the leaves, tug my pants free and quickly pull them on, and feel a soft, tickly lump pressing against my skin and a tingling across my bum cheeks which quickly escalates into a sharp stinging sensation, like TCP dabbed on an open cut, and moments later my bum starts to burn. Trying not to panic I yank my pants off and look inside. Clinging to the damp material is a red and yellow striped caterpillar, with tufts of black bristles standing up along its back. I kick my pants away and my panic starts to rise as the burning across my bum becomes more intense.

I briefly consider returning to the river to bathe the sting but then I notice that all my hasty scrabbling to enter the top of the chute has created a pool of liquid mud. I gratefully lower myself into it, sighing with relief as the cool mud soothes my skin. I move to and fro, sloshing about and digging myself deeper until the mud coats my shoulders and laps under my chin. Mosquitoes jig all around me but they're not biting, and I realise it's because they can't penetrate my mud shield, so I scoop up handfuls of mud and smear it all over my face, massaging it into my hair and scalp, pretending it's top-of-the-range insect-repellent shampoo.

With mud plugging my ears I can no longer hear the whining mosquitoes and I close my eyes.

My intention was to stay in the mud bath for a few minutes at most, but I must have dozed off for much longer than that because when I wake and try to open my eyes my eyelids are stuck together and the mud has turned cold and gluey. With some difficulty I manage to half open one eye and peer around, and the first thing I see is a pig. A hairy, Yoda-eared pig about five metres away down the slide, rolling around in the mud.

Not able to believe my eyes, I blink hard, cracking the mud coating both eyelids and look again. It's still there, and it's definitely a pig. A pig with a long snout and curved tusks, so a wild boar really. But still a pig, and still made of pork!

I glance at my spear, tantalisingly out of reach. There's no way I could reach it without alarming the pig, and anyway, as I take in the size of the beast I quickly realise how idiotic I'm being. It's me who's more in danger of being killed here, not the stocky, well-armed pig.

While I try to decide whether to make a break for it or wait for the pig to finish its wallowing, a bird cries in alarm and spooks it. The pig grunts and clambers from the mud and trots away, shaking its head and swishing its tail, still without having seen me.

Sighing with relief I wait until I'm sure the pig has gone before grabbing handfuls of grass and extracting myself from the mud, making a wet, sucking sound. The congealed mud on my face and shoulders cracks and falls off like chocolate cake icing, but it clings to the hairs on my legs, pinching my skin, and even though I know I should get on with hauling the heavy branch back to camp, then make the fire and change my bedding, I know I won't be able to sleep unless I wash it off first so I lower myself into the slide and try to push off. But since it's stopped raining the puny trickle of stream water isn't powerful enough to wet the chute any more and my descent is slow and uncomfortable. And it's nowhere near as much fun without Galaxy.

I plop into the river and tread water while I quickly wash the mud off and try to stop my mind summoning up visions of roast pork and crackling. Something glints in the sun. Something shiny and silver, and low in the sky. Something totally out of place. I climb onto the log jam to get a better look, and I hear it. A throbbing, regular tone, like a metal heartbeat, and my own heart jumps as I realise what it is. A helicopter! A miraculous, magnificent helicopter. They've come at last. The search team has found me! But then I realise. No. They haven't found me. Not yet. They're still too far away. They have no idea I'm here and if I stay where I am they'll never see me, not while I'm this far down and hidden by the overhanging trees. I have to get back to my camp site, with my *HELP* sign, and the tree-free sky, before the helicopter gets there. It's my only chance of being seen. But how can I get back in time? Even if I run as fast as I can along the riverbank it will take too long. And there's no way I can swim that far against the current.

I only have one option. I have to cut straight across the bend. Through the jungle. Barefoot. It's by far the shortest route and my only chance of reaching the sandspit in time. I scramble up the bank and pull on my T-shirt and pants, eating up precious seconds, but I can't bear the thought of being naked when I'm rescued. Then I run. I run as fast as I can through the undergrowth, ignoring the thorns and stones stabbing my feet and the sharp grass and brambles whipping my bare legs. I'm in luck, the foliage is nowhere near as dense as I feared and I'm covering the ground like a dog chasing a stick, panting hard and delirious with excitement. Upon reaching a clearing, a kind of motley green glade, I pause to check my bearings. Monkeys are howling nearby and I jump up and down and yell at them to shut up so I can listen for the helicopter.

There's a break in the squabbling and I can hear the reassuring throb of the helicopter, coming from the direction I'm facing. Thankfully I'm still heading the right way and it's much louder. I'm getting closer. I'm going to make it. I'm going to be saved! I quickly brush the wet hair out of my eyes and reach down to remove what feels like a vine wrapped around my ankle.

And I watch in disbelieving horror as first my feet, then my ankles, disappear into dark green moss. I try to lift them but as soon as my feet drop below the moss I start sinking quickly, and in a matter of seconds I'm up to my knees in clinging, cloying mud. I frantically try to yank my legs clear but they're held fast. Leaning forward, I push down hard on the ground in front of me to try to get some leverage, but my hands break straight through a thin crust of earth into thick mud beneath and my arms vanish past my wrists.

Quickly pulling my arms free I try again to lift my legs, but every time I make a move I sink deeper and the mud presses harder against me, as if I'm caught in a vice and the screw is tightening with every centimetre I sink. Forcing my hands deep into the mud packed against my legs I lock my fingers behind my right knee and pull, trying to raise my leg towards the surface, but it won't budge, and all I succeed in doing is panicking myself even further.

Already short of breath from running, I'm now wheezing badly. I have to calm down. I have to stop struggling. Linking my fingers behind my head I try to control my breathing while I scan around, searching for a way out.

But there are no trees or overhanging branches within reach and apart from the spongy moss the only vegetation I can see is a clump of reeds on my left.

I reach for the reeds, but even at full stretch my fingertips are still a hand's length away. I twist and bend at the waist and lean forward, pushing my chest so hard into the mud I can hardly breathe. But by holding my breath and straining as hard as I can, I just about touch the reeds. I grab a handful and pull. The blades are as sharp as knives and slice into my skin and I scream and let go. Blood seeps from deep cuts across my palms and they sting viciously; I know any further attempts will be incredibly painful. But I have no choice. By moving around so much to reach the reeds I have sunk even further and the mud is now past my waist and pressing punishingly hard against the bottom of my ribcage. I only have to sink another centimetre or two and the reeds will be out of reach. And by now the helicopter could be at the sandspit. I wipe the blood and grime from my palms on my T-shirt and grasp the reeds with both hands and pull. The pain is excruciating and the mud tries to suck me back in but I squeeze the reeds even tighter, twisting the blades between my fingers to get a better grip. I think I feel a slight movement in my waist and I pull even harder. This time I'm sure I've moved a bit more and I pull with all my might, ignoring the agony in my hands, and I hear a gurgling, sucking sound and suddenly the entire clump of reeds pulls free, with roots still attached, and I jerk backwards and sink even deeper into the mud.

I stare in horror at the clump of muddy reeds in my trembling, bloody hands, and I scream, and fling them as far away from me as I can, and as my scream dies I hear the helicopter. It's close. Very close. So close the downdraft from its rotor blades is swaying the treetops and I can feel the solid *thump-thump* of its engines vibrating the ground around me. In a few moments it will pass overhead. I cup my hands around my mouth and I yell, 'Here! I'm here!' as loud as I can, then furiously wave my hands above my head, even though I know there's no way anyone on board can hear me, or see me through the trees, and my movements will make me sink even further. But I can't help myself. I have to do something. In a matter of seconds the helicopter will be gone and if they don't see me now...

The helicopter banks away, the swaying trees slow and fall still, and the promising pulse of the engine dies, slowly fading as the rescue team heads downstream, following the course of the river, passing over the log pile I was standing on a few minutes ago.

The glade is eerily quiet. The monkeys have fled and all I can hear is my own heavy breathing, and the echo of rotor blades in my head. I cling to the sound, willing it to grow louder, and for the helicopter to turn around and come back and find me. But I know that isn't going to happen.

My aching arms drop and I slump forward and this time my chest doesn't even touch the ground. It can't. My futile attempts at being seen have resulted in me sinking even further and the mud is now halfway to my armpits, pressing hard against my ribcage and compressing my lungs.

All too soon even the shadow whisper of the helicopter's heartbeat is gone and all that's left is the sound of my wheezing breath and the bitter taste of despair. Total, utter despair.

I'm trapped. Helpless. I'll simply keep sinking and suffocate, buried alive. Or a predator will get me first. I'm finished. And I'm going to die here. Alone.

TWENTY-TWO

Dusk. I shiver and wrap my arms around my chest. As soon as the sun sets the temperature will plummet and my T-shirt will provide little protection from the cold. Worse still, nightfall will trigger the emergence of the jungle's nocturnal predators and with no spear or fire to deter them, I'm easy prey.

It doesn't take long for the torment to begin. Midges find me first. Hordes of them. They're so small I can't see them in the dull light but I can feel them biting every exposed inch of skin on my head and arms; feasting in silence and leaving a maddening itch.

I plaster mud over my arms and face and rake my muddy fingers through my hair to protect my scalp, like I did in the mud bath, but the midges are even more determined and persistent than the mosquitoes were and a few still manage to find the parts I can't protect;

the tiny strips of skin between my eyelashes, and inside my nostrils. My lips and inner ears.

Within minutes my ears feel like they're on fire and I want to slap and pinch them hard, and scream abuse at the midges. But I'm afraid that if I open my mouth the midges will feast on my lips and tongue and I daren't risk alerting any animals nearby. So I grit my teeth and try to roll my lips into my mouth instead, and dig out another handful of mud to coat my ears with. And as I do so I feel something hard and sharp digging into my left thigh.

Keeping my right hand free to swipe at the midges I force my left hand deep into the mud until my fingertips touch the solid object and I can grab it and twist it to and fro, until eventually it comes loose and I manage to work it up the back of my leg to the surface. Holding it close to my face I can see it's a bone. A big one. As long as my forearm, with a splintered end and a ball joint at the other. Probably an animal's leg bone. The remains of some previous victim. I grip the bone hard. It's useless against the midges but its solidness and weight are comforting. At least now I have a weapon.

That night is the worst I have ever known. And the longest. I'm so cold my teeth chatter uncontrollably and my jaw aches, and all I can think about is how I'm going to die. Not if. Or when. Just how. No moonlight penetrates the cloud-filled sky and in my tormented imagination every rustle and crack from the darkness signals the presence of a skulking creature impatiently watching me, waiting for me to fall asleep before it attacks. Perhaps my executioner will be a jaguar that picks up my scent and crushes my skull in its jaws, like a soft-boiled egg in an eggshell. Or a pack of wild pigs will find me and gore me to death. Or a snake or spider will strike, silent and unseen, and retreat to the blackness to wait and watch while I die a slow and agonising death.

Another rustle in the darkness, and the panic swells in my chest as the feeling of being watched intensifies. I can sense something, I'm sure of it; a bloodthirsty presence, lurking in the undergrowth. I'm getting hysterical now, I know I am, but I can't help it, and I can stay silent no longer. I pound the ground with my bone club and scream at the darkness, 'No! Go away. Whatever you are, go away!' It's not fair. I've done nothing to deserve this!

The jungle falls silent for a while, but then the rustling resumes, sporadic and terrifying. I wet myself.

I can't take this. I have to do something, anything to stem the terror savaging my mind. And it comes to me, and I do something I haven't done for years. I bow my head and I pray. I pray for a miracle. I pray that I die quickly.

TWENTY-THREE

Parrots wake me, screeching nearby.

My prayers went unanswered. I'm still alive.

The realisation that I've survived the night brings no relief. Just pain and hunger and a searing thirst. My legs ache as if they're encased in concrete and the cold night has compressed the mud around my chest so much that it's painfully difficult to breathe.

Nothing else has changed. I'm still going to die. All that's happened is the list of possibilities of how the jungle will kill me has grown, and now I can add a slow, lingering death from dehydration or starvation to the list.

By mid-morning I've scraped up all the moss within reach and sucked every last trace of moisture from it. But it's nowhere near enough to quench my thirst and the morning passes in a haze of pain and hopelessness.

And hunger. And thirst. Always thirst. Agonising, brain-shrivelling thirst, until sometime around noon when, with the blazing sun directly above me, and my head feeling as if it is about to burst into flame, it becomes clear what I can do. I can let go. I can simply let go and slip beneath the surface where it's cool and safe and the sun and the insects can't reach me. I can beat the jungle after all. I can win.

I raise my arms above my head and wriggle my upper body but I don't move. Not an inch. The same sun that's frying my brain has baked the mud solid and I'm held fast. I'm going nowhere. The jungle won't even let me kill myself.

And with this thought something crumbles in my mind. Some sort of mental barrier, and the memories come flooding back. I remember the crash. I remember the plane plunging and pitching, and the pounding rain. I remember the spluttering engine and the streaks of flaming oil lashing my window. I remember being frozen in my seat, too terrified to move while the plane juddered and lurched and luggage ricocheted around the cabin. I remember the force of the dive pinning me to the back of my chair and my fingers digging into the seat rests. I remember Dad yelling at me to buckle my seat belt and put my life jacket on. I remember using my life jacket as a pillow while I slept, and how it flew out of reach to the back of the plane. I remember unbuckling my seat belt earlier, to be more comfortable while I slept, even though I promised Dad I wouldn't.

I remember Dad undoing his seat belt and clawing his way across to me, bracing himself against the door handle while he buckled mine. I remember the look in his eyes as he took off his own life jacket and thrust it over my head. I remember grabbing handfuls of his shirt and clutching him tight and not letting him return to his own seat as the engine coughed and died and the plane plummeted. I remember the shirt ripping and Dad flying away from me as we slammed into the water.

The shock of recall is overwhelming. The brutal truth about what happened to Dad. The sickening realisation that he's dead. And it's my fault.

I thought the pain was bad before, when the helicopter left, but this is worse, much worse. It feels as if my ribs have been snapped in two and the jagged ends are being screwed into my heart. My chest heaves against the unyielding clay and I wheeze and blink uncontrollably, but I do not cry. I cannot. My body has no moisture left to spare for tears.

I have never felt such despair. Such misery. I want the jungle to finish me. I don't care how. I just want the pain to end. I raise my head and in a hoarse voice I scream, 'Do it. Do it now!' But I know I'm wasting my time. I'm condemned. Subject to the mercy of the jungle, and the jungle has no mercy. It wants me to suffer some more. To know I'm powerless, and I have been all along. It wants me to know it can snuff out my insignificant life any time it likes, just like I squash a mosquito, or crush the ticks burrowing into my skin.

The scream has exhausted me, and it feels like my lungs have ruptured from the effort. I don't even have enough strength left to hold my head up and it drops to my chest. So I do the one thing I still have control over. The one thing the jungle can't take away from me. The only thing that makes any sense.

I close my eyes and I pray. But this time I don't pray for death or for the pain to end.

I pray for the impossible instead. I pray that Dad is alive. I pray he makes it home to Mum.

And with thoughts of Mum now filling my head I remember the last time we spoke, and every word she said. I remember the look in her eyes when she made me promise I would be careful, and do what Dad told me to, and come home safe. And I promised.

I pummel the ground, and try to scream, but my throat is too dry, my tongue too swollen. I do not want to die. I want to live! I so badly want to live. I have to. I have to make it back to Mum. I have to keep my promise.

It starts to rain.

Lightly at first, pattering through the trees. I throw my head back and stretch my mouth wide, and frantically gulp the cold water. The shower quickly becomes a deluge, drumming on my head and shoulders and pooling around me. Lightning flares through the canopy and I can see the clearing has been transformed into a shallow pool, and even in my deranged state I realise the water level will soon rise above my head and I will drown, or it will liquefy the clay encasing me and I will slip beneath the surface and choke to death as my lungs fill with rancid mud. And my body will never be found. And as the rain falls hard and heavy, and thunder quakes the air I make another promise. I make a vow on my own life that if I can just escape this watery tomb I will find a way to get out of the jungle and make it home to Mum. I swear I won't leave her alone.

Thrusting my hands through the water, I press down into the sludge, trying to lever my legs out, but my body still won't budge and the effort sends a stab of pain shooting up my spine.

The water level keeps rising fast and there's so much rain hammering down and rebounding into my face that every breath I take seems more liquid than air. I never imagined the sky could hold so much water. Or release it with such force.

But the battering seems to help. It flushes and revives my brain. From a distant corner of my mind I hear a faint voice telling me to calm down, to control my emotions and concentrate. And I know the voice. I know it's Dad! 'Take a deep breath and calm down,' he says again, in his measured, steady voice. 'You can do this, you just have to focus and find a way.' And I so badly want to believe him, to believe he's right, so I squint through the driving rain for any sliver of hope, anything that might be of help. Another bolt of lightning splits the darkness and I can see the tip of my bone club sticking up through the water, and I have an idea.

I grab the bone and ram its jagged end into the spot where the reeds were, and pull. The bone tilts and pops free almost immediately and I let out a cry of anguish before trying again. This time the bone stays in place, but my wet hands slip free and I scream. I try for a third time, cautiously pulling on the bone, checking the resistance. It holds firm so I clamp both hands tight around the shaft and pull. Blood pumps from the cuts on my palms and a searing pain shoots up my spine, and I let go and howl again, gutted by my failure. It's no good. I can't do this!

But I have to. So I wrench the bone free and drive it back into the mud, deeper this time. I feel it snag and catch, and I pull, and I think I feel my legs move. Leaning as far forward as I can I pull again, and this time I'm sure I feel a slight give around my waist.

Clenching my shoulders I pull again. Another stab of pain shoots up my spine and it takes all my willpower not to let go, but I know if I do I'm finished. I will sink further into the mud and the bone will be out of my reach.

With my hands still wrapped tightly around the bone, I take a deep breath and press my face into the water, burying my nose in the mud. And I pull. With strength I never knew I had, I pull. With blood pouring from my hands and my lungs screaming for air, I pull. With the muscles in my arms threatening to tear in two and my shoulders feeling like they will pop out of their sockets, I pull. With my spine stretched to breaking point and the blackness of the water seeping into my brain, I pull. With a fire blazing in my chest, I pull.

My legs move, and I rise just enough to be able to lift my face clear of the water and breathe again.

Now I can scream while I pull. So I do. I scream louder than I ever have before. I scream abuse at the jungle, and the storm, and the mud, and my puny body.

I scream with all the rage and volume I can muster. The sound comes from deep within me, from my core, rising through my blazing chest and erupting from my mouth in a howl of defiance. It's a sound I didn't know I was capable of producing. A sound like no sound I've ever made before. I will not die here, not like this. I refuse to! To die means breaking another promise and leaving Mum alone. It means giving up and letting Dad down, and I won't do that. Not again.

So I pull. I pull and I scream.

And with a sudden lurch my waist rises a few centimetres from the sinkhole. I pull again, now able to gain some leverage by digging my elbows into the mud below the water and pushing down, and another few centimetres of my body slides clear.

I don't know how many times I repeat the same excruciating action, or how long it takes me to reclaim my body from the pit, but centimetre by impossible centimetre, that's what I do. Snorting and spluttering. Straining every fibre and sinew until my feet slide from the hole and I can drag my leaden legs clear, and slither out of that cold muddy grave. I grab the first tree

I reach, wrap my arms around its trunk and grip it as tightly as I can in case the mud rises up to swallow me.

The rain eases, gently massaging my body and washing the mud away. Then it stops. My racing heart slows to normal speed. I let go of the tree and I stand. Blood flows back into my legs, inflamed with pins and needles, and I accept the pain. I welcome it. It means I'm alive. It means I didn't give up. I can only manage two faltering steps before my legs buckle and I collapse. But I will not stay down. I don't have to. I'm stronger than this.

I stand. I stand because I know I can. I stand because I have to.

Bone club in hand, I take a last look at the still, moonlit pool behind me. Then I spit into the black water and turn and walk away.

I have a promise to keep.

PART THREE

TWENTY-FOUR

The helicopter isn't coming back.

However much I don't want to believe it, I know it's true, and the longer I stay here, the greater the chances are that something is going to get me – animal, insect, disease, injury or starvation, whatever. It's raining more often as well, making it harder to keep the fire alight. But at least the storm that almost drowned me in the mud pit also dumped loads of wood on the sandspit, so I don't have to spend so much time searching for fuel. And with any luck somewhere amongst the driftwood I will find the material I need to complete my task – timbers to build a raft.

Walking out is not an option. There are too many snakes and other deadly things in the jungle, and there are no trails to follow. As soon as I lost sight of the river I wouldn't know which direction to head in. Even if I did have a vague idea, I don't have a compass, not that I know how to use one anyway, and since the sun isn't visible through the dense canopy, I couldn't use it to navigate by either, so there would be nothing to prevent me from going round in circles. And I won't risk ending up deep in the jungle without a source of drinking water. No. Heading into the jungle is simply too dangerous. My only possible escape route is the river.

Even with its piranhas, caimans and rapids, the river is still the least worst of two crap options. Anyway, I don't have a choice. No one's coming to get me and if I stay here I will die. I got cocky, thinking I could beat the jungle. Lazy too, neglecting the fire and my *HELP* sign. I realise that now, and once the relief of escaping from the pit had faded, I spent most of yesterday and last night feeling massively depressed and pissed off with myself. But I've finally got it through my thick head that it's a complete waste of time beating myself up over things I can no longer do anything about. I have to stay positive and tell myself it's not too late. I have to believe that if I work harder than I ever have before and I'm not careless, or too hasty, and stay focused on just one thing – building a raft – then I will make it out of here. There can be no more delays or diversions. No more time squandered on improving the camp site. No more mistakes. From this moment on, everything I do has to be done with only one aim in sight – to get out of the jungle, and back home to Mum.

I pick up my rod and the three piranhas I've caught and take another hopeful look at Otter Rock. There's been no sign of Galaxy or his mother since my return the night before last. I guess they must have moved on, probably to reach higher ground before the rainy season arrives. Maybe. I'm trying hard not to think about them too much, but the truth is I desperately miss their company, Galaxy's especially, even if a small part of me is secretly relieved he's not here. I can't afford any distractions and I'm not looking forward to saying goodbye. So I try to console myself with the knowledge that, however much I miss him, at least this is Galaxy's home and he's with his mum. Now it's time for me to go to home and be with mine.

TWENTY-FIVE

The next two days pass in a sweaty grind of driftwood sorting and hauling, fishing and foraging for provisions. I'm permanently exhausted and filthy, apart from when it rains. My bed stays unchanged and mouldy. I don't bathe. My teeth are unbrushed and furry. I don't take a break at midday, and although I'm hungry all the time I barely pause to eat until after the sun's gone down. I've lost so much weight even my pants are too big for me now and the elastic's shot anyway, so I go naked all the time – apart from occasionally wearing my trainers, when I need their protection from ants and thorns.

While I don't bother with the smoke signals any more I do spend some time coaxing the fire back to life in the evenings, when it's not raining, to cook and eat as many fish as I can. All this physical work gives me an insatiable appetite, and I know I need to consume as much protein as possible to build my strength for the raft trip. And after finding more large paw prints by the stream I really don't want to be without the light and security of my fire. But despite the exhaustion, the rain and Galaxy's absence, overall I'm feeling pretty positive. Doing something constructive instead of waiting for something to happen feels good. It feels like I'm in control.

After many hours of boring sorting, I have the material I need to build a raft – three small trunks and two thick branches, and a pile of bamboo poles to provide extra buoyancy. Hauling them all to a launch site on the riverbank has taken every ounce of strength I possess and most of the skin from my knuckles. If Mum had heard the swear words spewing out of me over the last couple of days I'd be grounded for the rest of my life.

Thankfully, gathering provisions has been much easier. The piranhas are as ravenous as ever, and amongst the debris washed up by the storm I've found some lightning-severed branches laden with Brazil nut pods, and a few metres along from the Joshua Tree one of the trees I hadn't taken much notice of before has produced a crop of mango-like fruit, the size of big lemons, with green rind and sweet, amber-coloured pulp. I've even collected and sun-dried a few of the fig-like fruit I found washed up on the shore, as emergency rations, figuring my stomach's tough enough to handle them now, although I can only hope I don't ever have to eat them. I have no idea how many days I will have to spend on the raft so I'm determined to take as much food as I can cram into the pockets and tied-off legs of my jeans, and wrap in my pants and T-shirt. Anything I find or catch along the way will be a bonus.

Only two stumbling blocks remain in the way of my departure, but they're big ones: how can I tie the logs together? And how can I carry clean drinking water on the raft? Making a raft looks so straightforward when Bear Grylls does it, but I don't have his expertise, or strength, or machete, and my attempts to strip tree bark and braid vines to make rope have been beyond pathetic. As for transporting fresh stream water to drink, the truth is I may have no option but to rely on rainfall and the dirty river instead.

Placing another log from my stack of raft rejects on the fire, I yawn, and shiver, more from tiredness than the cold. It's been another long and tiring day, but a productive one. My food store is growing rapidly and as soon as I've solved the log-tying problem I can go. I should be pleased with myself. I should be happy. But I'm not. The truth is I have no idea what the river may have in store for me. And even more worryingly, there's still no sign of the otters.

TWENTY-SIX

Sometime during a restless night I'm convinced I've come up with a brilliant solution to my log-tying problem. I'll use my shoelaces!

But one quick check at first light is all it takes to let me know what a stupid idea it is. Firstly the knot where I've tied them onto the rod is so tight it's impossible to unpick, secondly the laces are badly frayed and look like they could snap at any moment, and thirdly they're nowhere near long enough to go around five logs, let alone the bamboo poles as well.

Not the greatest of starts to the day. I will think about it some more while I'm fishing. And hoping the laces don't snap.

By midday I've caught four good-sized fish and lost at least six more by falling asleep, so I decide to stop fishing and head back to camp for a nap.

With a breeze blowing through the camp site, a potent fishy and fruity aroma hits me while I'm still at least ten paces away and I realise that for the first time since the crash I have enough food. More than enough really. My pile of mangoes (or whatever they are) is so high that the ones on the bottom are starting to go off and ferment, my hoard of fish is deteriorating rapidly in the heat, and everything is teeming with ants. Up close the fishy odour is pretty foul and overpowering, there are flies everywhere, and my musty bed appears to be alive with millions of red mites, so I quickly place my fish on the pile and return to the shade of the crooked tree to rest. I'll deal with the mess later.

Before I lie down I slowly scan up and down the far bank as far as I can see, then check Otter Rock. There's still no sign of Galaxy or his mother. I try to tell myself not to worry, to convince myself that their absence is a good thing, and simply means they've moved on. But the truth is I've changed my mind, and I do want to see them, especially Galaxy. I need to know he's OK, and I'm a little hurt to think he'd leave without saying goodbye.

TWENTY-SEVEN

Rain wakes me. Tapping on my eyelids and rudely interrupting a dream where I'm tobogganing with Galaxy and we're shrieking with delight. Dad's just given our sledge a shove down a hill smothered in freshly fallen snow, and Mum's waiting at the bottom. I squeeze my eyelids tight and try to stay in the dream for a little longer, at least until we reach the bottom, but the annoying rain jolts me back to the present. Judging by the dull light and cool air it's nearly dusk. I must have slept all afternoon. Damn! Even if the rain stops now there isn't enough sunlight left to relight the fire, and without it I can't cook my fish.

I wipe the rain from my face and peer across the river at Otter Rock. Still no sign of the otters, so I leave the shade of the crooked tree and head back to camp. And can hardly believe my eyes.

Even in the dim light of dusk I can see I've had an uninvited and greedy visitor.

My food store has been decimated. All the mangoes have gone or been partially eaten and the rinds scattered around. The fish have all been devoured too, or had bites taken out of them and their bony remains trampled into the dirt. My bedding and pile of kindling for the fire are strewn everywhere. For a moment my mood brightens and my pulse quickens as I hope the otters are responsible, but as I pick my way through the soggy mess I can see sausage-sized turds littering the ground, tufts of wiry black hair snagged in the trunk of the Joshua Tree, and dozens of distinctive trotter prints in the damp earth. There's no mistaking the identity of the intruder – a pig! The fermenting fruit must have drawn it in, like a fly to rotting flesh.

I'm furious. And I don't want to think about what might have happened if I'd been asleep on my bed when it arrived. But, gutted as I am by the mess and the loss of my provisions, I'm even more worried that my life jacket isn't where I left it wedged in the crook of the Joshua Tree. I can't see it anywhere.

Frantically digging through strewn bedding and ruined food, I eventually find it covered in wet ash by the fire. I unseal the pocket and grunt in relief when I see Dad's watch parts are still inside. Thankfully they appear to have escaped further damage, and the fire glass is still safely tucked away in the other pocket.

After wiping off the sticky charcoal coating, I cram the life jacket back in the Joshua Tree, making sure it's secure, then spend the last few minutes of fading daylight salvaging what little I can of my spoiled provisions. It doesn't amount to much – a few half-eaten piranhas and a handful of Brazil nuts. No mangoes, and Porky Pig has even gobbled up all the dried figs. There will be no supper for me tonight. But I have no appetite anyway. In fact I feel sick at the thought of the pig invading my space, stealing my food and trashing my home. Now it knows there's food here, it could return at any time.

And there's absolutely nothing I can do about it. I don't have the time or the energy to set up camp somewhere else or build a fence to keep it out. What if I ambush it? Bait a trap with fruit and hide in the branches of the Joshua Tree, then drop and stab it with my spear or bludgeon it to death with my bone club. Yeah right, like that's going to happen! However much I try to think about something else, anything else, I keep picturing the wicked tusks on the wild boar I saw at Galaxy's mudslide, and then I think about the big paw prints in the mud by the stream. If a pig can find me then a jaguar can too. I've run out of time. I'll just have to risk my shoelaces and reduce the raft from five logs to three or two.

It's time to go.

TWENTY-EIGHT

Tired and aching, I crawl out of my soggy bed in the pre-light of dawn, impatient for the sun to rise to warm me so I can gather more fruit, catch some fish, finish the raft, and be on my way.

Catching fish shouldn't be a problem, and thankfully there are still some mangoes left on the tree. But even though I'm anxious to leave, there's something I have to do first. I have to make one last trip to the otters' mudslide. One last attempt to find Galaxy.

The sun appears. I sit and slip one trainer on and as I lift the second one something small and black falls to the ground. At first I assume it's a beetle. But then it rights itself and rears up and I realise it's a scorpion, jet black, with its sting-tipped tail cocked and claws flung wide, threatening me. Threatening me! I'm ten thousand times its size and could crush it in an instant.

I snort with disdain and raise my trainer to kill it, but it's already scrabbled away into the undergrowth.

I grab my spear. Then decide to leave it. I'll run faster without it.

I reach the mudslide in good time, and kneel to extract a thorn from my trainer when I hear something, a muffled hollering noise, coming from the jungle. I peer in the direction the sound came from, but I can't see anything alarming and I decide my tired and overanxious mind must be playing tricks on me. I stand and walk towards the top of Galaxy's slide when I hear the noise again, closer this time – sharp cries and barks, and it's suddenly clear what sort of animal is heading my way, and fast – monkeys!

Memories of my previous encounter with monkeys fill my head and I spin round and get ready to run. And stop. I can't leave yet. Not before I've done what I came here to do. Not before I've checked for any sign of the otters. So I decide to hide instead, and hope the monkeys change direction before they reach me.

Quickly burrowing into the foliage, I crouch down and pull fern fronds over my head, feeling acutely exposed and vulnerable in my nakedness and cursing myself for leaving my spear behind.

The bush has barely stopped shaking before I see a flash of gold dart through the branches of the trees nearby and disappear into a cavity of the dead tree above me – the golden lion tamarin!

Seconds later the first monkey arrives, crashing through the canopy. He's huge, with massive muscular shoulders and a silver-grey back and chest. Four smaller monkeys follow close behind, and halt in the higher branches of the tree alongside the one I'm hiding beneath, the same one I climbed to reach the tamarin's nest.

The big monkey howls, opening his mouth wide to display broken brown front teeth as he glowers at the gang of four following him, warning them to back off. Then he raises a fistful of leaves to his flaring nostrils and inhales, and swings across to the tamarin's nest, directly above me.

Pressing his cheek flat against the trunk, the big monkey reaches into the tamarin's nest and yanks out the golden ball of fur. The tamarin squirms and trills like a bat and tries to bite the ape's stumpy fingers, but the monkey grips it firmly in both hands, raises it to its mouth, and bites into the tamarin's stomach. The tamarin screams in agony as blood spurts from the wound, and its tail whips to and fro and wraps around a branch, anchoring it. But the big monkey easily pulls the tail free and rips another chunk of fur and flesh from his helpless prey, and sits back and chews it, glaring at the four monkeys in the neighbouring tree who are going crazy now, screeching and bouncing up and down on the branches, but they dare not move any closer.

The tamarin's screams cut me to the bone and I want to burst out of my hiding place and pelt the monkey with sticks and stones and yell at it to stop, to let the tamarin go. But I can't. It's already too late for the tamarin and I'm petrified the pack will turn on me if I do. So I clamp my hands over my ears instead, to try to block out the tamarin's cries as the monkey eats it alive, casually crunching bones and tearing flesh until it bites through the tamarin's neck, severing its spine, and the screaming stops.

Bloodlust sated, the big monkey drops the tamarin's carcass and swings away, leaving the others to fight over the once beautiful creature's remains, hanging broken and bloody on a bough.

I stay where I am for an hour or more, unable to move while the monkeys squabble over scraps of fur and bone, telling myself over and over again that there was nothing I could do to save the tamarin. That it would have been suicidal to try. But however hard I try, I can't silence the nasty, sneering voice telling me I should have done something. Anything. I should have at least tried. Telling me what I already know. That I'm a coward, a pretender, and I've been found out.

Only when I'm certain the monkeys have gone and I can stand the cramps in my legs no longer, do I emerge from my hiding place, sick to my stomach. I'm ashamed and desperate to get back to my camp site. But there's still something I have to do first.

I'm three or four paces away from the slide when I come across the first signs of a fight – snapped branches, blood-splattered leaves and deep gouges in the mud. Heart pounding, I take two more steps towards the slide, and that's when I see the big paw prints in the mud, the same type I've seen by the stream at the sandspit. There are clumps of fur, caked in blood, and a track of bloody flattened grass heading into the jungle. As if a heavy object has been dragged away. A wild pig perhaps. Or an otter.

TWENTY-NINE

I should be fishing, and sorting out the raft and getting out of this hell. But I'm not. I'm standing at the river's edge instead, just below the rapids, trying to summon up the courage to wade in and swim to the other side.

It seemed so simple this morning – gather fruit, catch fish, finish the raft and leave. But that was before my trip to the mudslide, and the realisation that if the clumps of bloody fur belonged to Galaxy's mother, and she was killed and Galaxy survived, then he would do exactly the same thing that I would. He would head for home. This morning I had no clues as to where he might be. This morning there were no cackling vultures, circling above a point on the other side of the river, steadily spiralling lower and lower. But there are now.

I wade in.

The riverbed is firm underfoot but the strong current tugs at my legs, and I swim as hard and as fast as I can, focusing on one stroke at a time, then the next. Swimming across the current is far more tiring than I had expected it to be and I'm struggling badly, swallowing litres of water, and by the time my feet touch the bottom on the other side I'm a long way downstream from the vultures, well below Otter Rock. Scrambling ashore, I cough up mouthfuls of dirty water and take a moment to clear my nostrils and catch my breath before making my way upstream.

Fish bones and crab shells litter the ground around Otter Rock, and the mud is studded with paw prints, but they're all jumbled up and it's impossible to tell how old they are. I decide to follow a path that appears to be more worn than others, and leads upriver, towards the vultures.

The entrance to the otters' holt is hidden beneath a mesh of flowering vines entwined in the roots of a fallen tree on the riverbank, and without the vultures spiralling overhead I would never have found it.

Pushing through the tangle of flowers, I lean forward as far as I can, until my face is nestling amongst the purple blooms. I call Galaxy's name, and make the burring squeak of greeting, and listen, and hear nothing. No sounds of movement or squeak in response. Just silence. I lean further out, to where rain has dissolved some of the earth, clear my throat and make the *To me!* whistle, the one I spent so many hours practising. Still nothing. Wetting my lips I whistle again, and it's better this time, fuller and more distinct. And I hear it, above the sound of the river and the cackling vultures. There's the faintest chirp in return.

'Galaxy. Galaxy!' I cry, and attack the earth forming the roof of the holt with my bare hands, crushing flowers, snapping roots, and ripping through vines and mud. My fingers are soon stained yellow with pollen and torn and bleeding from thorns. But I keep tearing and digging, barely feeling the cuts, only pausing when my throat gets too clogged with thick dust to continue, and I cough and spit and call Galaxy's name. I am instantly re-energised when I hear his faint mew in reply.

After a few minutes I break through the earth and thorny crust to a layer of grass and dead reeds which is much easier to dismantle. Quickly tearing a hole in the lining, I lean forward and press my face into it. Hot and pungent air wafts up, and I splutter and spit, and turn my head to take a deep breath of fresh air before lowering it into the opening again. At first I can see nothing through the swirling dust cloud, and my mouth is too dry for me to whistle, so I call Galaxy's name instead, in a rasping voice. In a far corner of the gloom something moves. Curled up in a ball and half buried beneath dislodged mud and vines, Galaxy is virtually invisible except for a smudge of paleness from the white bib on his throat. I call to him again, more softly this time, and he raises his head at the sound of my voice. I reach down to him, and gently lift his limp body through the hole in the earth.

He's filthy. And stinks. His eyes are glued shut with crud but he still squints in the harsh light and buries his face in his paws. I turn my back to shield him from the bright sun, and hug him tightly against my wheezing chest. He's so skinny I can feel the curve of his ribs pressing against his skin, and I gently brush the dirt and vines from his body and stroke his head and neck, and he makes a burring noise in response and nuzzles his face deep into the crook of my arm.

I carry Galaxy to the river and sit cross-legged with him in the shallows, gently rocking him in my lap while he dips his head and feverishly gulps the water. When he's drunk his fill, he licks the insides of his wrists and shakily draws them across his eyes to clean them and the crusty guck falls away. After blinking hard a number of times Galaxy looks up at my dusty face and I can see the bewilderment and alarm in his eyes. He kicks against my legs and wriggles out of my lap, his sharp claws catching my thighs. I cry out but by the time I'm over the shock and I realise the scratches are not deep, Galaxy's gone. I can't see him anywhere but I can hear him. He's returned to the holt and he's mewing for his mother.

I take two paces towards the holt and stop. However much I want to help him, I know Galaxy's confused and frightened and I don't dare risk alarming him again. I have to give him some time to come to terms with this sudden change in his situation, to remember I'm his friend and he can trust me. A short while later Galaxy's head breaks the surface in the shallows halfway between me and the holt. He's chirping anxiously, bobbing and swivelling his head every few seconds to look at me and then back at the holt, and I realise he doesn't know what to do. Of course he doesn't! He's just a pup and he's used to Mum making all his decisions for him. Now he needs me to help him decide.

Well, I can't rush him, but I can't stay here either, and neither can Galaxy. If he crawls back into that holt again he will simply curl up and die there. Or a jaguar or caiman will discover the hole I ripped in the roof and kill him. Or the vultures will get him. His only chance is to come with me. The sooner I get us both back to my camp site the better.

So I do the only thing I can think of. I wade into the river and face him, arms spread wide, and I make the *To me!* whistle. But Galaxy keeps bobbing in the water, anxiously mewing and twisting his head, torn between me and his home. Something brushes against my leg and I lose it. That's it! I'm out of here. I've done all I can. It's up to Galaxy now.

I spin round and kick hard. When I'm a few body lengths from the shore Galaxy starts to follow me, trailing a few metres behind, chittering loudly. This time the current works in my favour, carrying me downstream towards my camp site, and I make the return crossing in half the time.

By the time we reach the sandspit and I drag my aching body up and out of the water, it's as if Galaxy has crossed a mental barrier as well as a physical one. Bounding past me, he shakes himself. Then he trots up and down, sniffing and scratching, before sitting back on his haunches and calling to me in a completely different tone from before, a pleading and insistent call. I recognise the cry. It's the *Give me food!* demand. He's hungry. I remember how he seemed to eat almost non-stop when he was with his mother, and I have no idea when he ate last.

So I stand and acknowledge his demand with a chirp in response, then run to camp to fetch some mangoes. Galaxy wolfs down the three I bring him and begs for more, but I've never seen him eat fruit before and I'm worried that such a large amount of rich food might be too much for his empty stomach to handle, so I return to camp to grab my fishing rod and head for the river. Galaxy follows close behind, chirping away and huffing impatiently, as if to hurry me along. Thankfully the piranhas are around and hungry, and I land a fish with each of my first three casts. Galaxy quickly devours them, and the next two as well, until he calls a halt at fish number six and starts to half-heartedly clean himself. But he falls asleep almost immediately, stretched out in the shade of the crooked tree.

I try to focus on my fishing, but I miss loads of bites by turning my head to check on him every few seconds or so. When I've caught another six piranhas I whistle to Galaxy to wake him, and head back to camp, laughing out loud as Galaxy tries to catch the fish swinging from my shoelace. I'm full of the most wonderful feeling of relief that my friend is alive and uninjured. And no longer alone.

THIRTY

That night, while Galaxy is busy chewing my wooden bowl, I make him a bed of leafy branches a couple of metres from mine, still in the warm radius of the fire but safely out of spark-spitting range, and I place a juicy mango on the leaves to tempt him, before lying down on my own bed to take the weight off my legs and allow the warmth of the fire to soothe my aching limbs. Galaxy smells the mango and plonks himself down on the leaves to eat it, and when he's finished he plays with the stone for a while, juggling it between his paws, then washes his face and lies down, facing me, head on paws, and eyes wide open.

I haven't had a moment's rest all day and after the two previous sleepless nights I can barely keep my eyes open. So I stretch, and roll onto my back but I feel my heartbeat quicken as Galaxy crawls towards me, closer and closer, until I can feel his breath on my ribs and smell his fish- and mango-scented fur. He circles three times before settling down next to me, legs tucked, tail wrapped around his belly, and paws curled over his eyes, with just his whiskers poking out. His back is warm and soft against my side and sends a surge of emotion through my chest. It's been a long time since I've felt the touch of a warm body, the reassuring pulse of another heartbeat, and I hadn't realised how much I'd missed it until now.

Rolling onto my side, I carefully raise my knees and curl my body to encircle him. Then I bend my arm around his tucked legs and cradle his head in my hand. As he pushes his back tighter against me I suddenly realise that the last few nights spent alone without his mother must have been hell for him. I gently stroke his rich velvet fur and softly tell him he's safe now, and there's nothing to be afraid of, until my head sinks into the leaves and I can keep my eyes open no longer.

Galaxy half-wakes many times during the night, sometimes with his body tensed and twisted, eyelids twitching, gums drawn back and claws flexing. Other times I hear him whimpering, his voice full of pain and sadness, and I know he's pining for his mother. So I stroke him, and curl more tightly around him, and tell him everything will be all right, until his body relaxes and his breathing is deep and regular once more. I tell him I'll look after him. I tell him my name.

THIRTY-ONE

For the next forty-eight hours Galaxy barely leaves my side. Which is fine with me. Even the most tedious tasks are fun when he's around. Apart from when I try to go to the toilet, that is. One of his favourite games is to hide in the undergrowth and leap out before I've finished, then bark with glee and race around my legs until I walk back to camp as fast as I can while he nips at my heels.

So this morning I waited until he was engrossed in his usual round of inspecting everything in camp before I sneaked away, leaving him to sniff, probe, shake, lick and taste each and every one of the few objects I possess – my now chewed-up wooden bowl, bone club and spear. My armoury of piranha jaws. My T-shirt, trainers and belt. Even my minging jeans get a good sniff and lick. But his favourite item by far is my fishing rod, which is hardly surprising I guess, seeing as it's seeped in fish blood and must be as irresistible to an otter as a leg of lamb is to a dog. But unfortunately for Galaxy I quickly sussed that his powerful jaws could snap the shaft with ease, and with two hungry mouths to feed I need the rod more than ever. So I keep it well out of his reach, high in the branches of the Joshua Tree, along with my trainers, since they started going walkabout too. I've wedged the life jacket even higher still, to keep Dad's watch and the precious fire glass out of his reach, and to prevent him ripping the jacket to pieces.

And it hasn't taken long to discover that as well as being unbelievably curious, Galaxy can be outrageously demanding as well, and when he's in his 'Give me attention' mood there's no way I can ignore him. Only when his demands have been met in full and he falls asleep do I get a chance to catch up on my chores: fetching wood, stoking the fire, gathering fruit and snails, shelling nuts or fishing. Mostly fishing.

Returning to camp, I spot Galaxy straight away, crouched on top of the log pile – his personal playground and the first place I check when yet another possession goes missing. But for once he's not hiding something, or stripping bark with his teeth to search for juicy grubs. Instead he's chomping his way through an emerald green beetle and grunting with delight as he does so.

I retrieve my fishing rod and whistle *To me!* and Galaxy leaps from the top of the pile to join me. With a regular supply of fish, fruit and nuts, Galaxy's body is starting to fill out, his fur is regaining its silky lustre and he smells like freshly mown grass again. But I decide he still needs fattening up with more fish, and to catch fish I need my shoelaces. The raft will have to wait.

THIRTY-TWO

By the morning of the third day since I found him, Galaxy has regained enough confidence to re-enter the river on his own, timidly at first, always staying within a few metres of the shore and repeatedly checking where I am and calling me to join him and play. His persistent pleas are impossible to resist for long so I decide to try playing throw and catch with him instead, which, if he gets it, will at least allow me to stay on dry land while hopefully tiring him out.

With a stack of a dozen small mangoes by my side, I sit cross-legged on the riverbank, and whistle to Galaxy to join me. Holding a mango high in the air so he can see it, I swing it backwards and forwards a few times before lobbing it underarm into the river, and reach for a second one, hoping I don't run out of fruit before he gets the idea. But before my probing fingers have even separated another mango from the pile, Galaxy has leaped from the bank, dived and resurfaced with the first one clasped in his mouth, and instead of floating on his back and eating it he swims to shore, drops it on the ground and looks up at me in anticipation. I'm astonished, and seriously impressed. I throw the next one twice as far as the first, and while it's still flying through the air Galaxy is swimming hard and fast out towards it, tracking the mango's progress, and mere seconds after it plops into the water he emerges a few metres downstream of where it entered, with water pouring off his polished head and the fruit held firmly in his teeth. Incredible! I sneakily fake throwing the next one, then lob it into the shallows, while his back is turned, and before the ripples have reached the shore Galaxy's spun round, dived and found it. And I clap, and cheer, and spend the next half an hour marvelling at the sheer speed of his reflexes.

He doesn't get a perfect score though, only eleven out of twelve, although to be fair it's hardly his fault seeing as I eat the last mango.

By the afternoon Galaxy's starting to venture further from shore, gliding out into midstream to investigate every piece of driftwood, or heading off to explore the riverbank further downstream. But every time he dives he soon surfaces to check I'm still sat on the riverbank watching him. And I always am.

Even though I know Galaxy is as at home in the river as he is on land, my stomach still clenches and my skin goes cold each time I lose sight of him, or I can't see any puffs of mud or silver bubbles to tell me where he is. If I think he's strayed too far or I can't take the stress any longer, I make the *To me!* whistle and he quickly swims back, runs out of the river and bounds up to me. Chirping joyfully, he'll lick my hands and face and squirm all over my feet as if we have been apart for weeks, before shaking furiously, showering me with water. But I don't mind his soppiness or the sticky feet. It's always a relief to have him back, and anyway when he's finished twirling and twisting, his fur sticks out so much he looks as cute and cuddly as a fluffy toy and I can't help but laugh.

Later that afternoon I reluctantly decide I can't face another night tossing and turning on my mouldy bed so as hard as it is to do, I leave Galaxy exploring the river while I head back to camp to change the bedding.

After grabbing armfuls of fresh leafy branches I stare down at the damp and decaying leaves of my old mattress, knowing I should remove them and dump them on the fire while I clear the area of insects and let the earth dry out. But that will take a while and I can't help thinking I've already been away from Galaxy for too long, so I simply chuck the new branches on top of the old and jog back to where I left him and start whistling.

When he doesn't immediately swim into view I panic; running up and down the riverbank, whistling hard and calling his name. Moments later he appears, loping back along the track from Snail Rock. Relief washes over me, and then surprise when I see a catfish flapping in his mouth. I've never seen Galaxy catch his own food before – up until now his mum or I have done all the fishing for him. As he draws closer, Galaxy's squeak of greeting is muffled by the mouthful of fish, but this time instead of his usual puppy-dog antics he halts a few metres away from me and flops down, holds the fish upright between his front paws and starts to eat it, crunching through the head first, popping the eyes and grinding the cheekbones to pulp, then gulping the fleshy belly, and in between mouthfuls I can hear him huffing in satisfaction. It's not a big fish and a bottom-grubbing catfish is undoubtedly much easier to catch than a piranha, but I'm almost certain it's the first fish Galaxy's ever caught and I swear there's a swagger to his walk as he tosses the last morsel down his throat and lopes away. I feel like I should say something but I'm grinning too hard and I'm far too emotional to speak. Galaxy's caught his first fish. His mum would be so proud. I know I am.

Sometime later, towards twilight, I'm collecting snails when I hear Galaxy approach, his squeak of greeting muffled like before. The catfish he's caught this time is much bigger, almost as long as my arm. I whistle in admiration, expecting Galaxy to simply sit and devour his catch like before. But instead he walks right up to me, drops the fish on the ground, retreats a little way back and lies down and pants, with his chin resting on his outstretched paws and eyes shining up at me.

Confused, I look down at the slowly gulping catfish and then at Galaxy, blinking and chirping away, as if waiting for me to do something. Perhaps he wants me to finish it off, or say something? But then I look at his beaming face again and I get it. The catfish is for me. It's a gift.

I keep my eyes on Galaxy as I slowly extend my hand and close my fingers around the catfish. As I do so Galaxy jumps to his feet and I snatch my hand back, alarmed that I may have misread the situation, and wary of his bone-crunching teeth. But Galaxy merely stands on all fours and grunts, and nods his head, and I pick up the catfish and lift it to my face and sniff, like an otter would. It stinks. And it's covered in slime. Somehow I resist the urge to vomit and drop it, and I grunt and murmur appreciatively instead, and lick my peeling lips. 'Yummy,' I say. 'Delicious. Thank you, Galaxy. Thank you and well done.' Galaxy raises himself on his hind legs and chuckles in response. Then he turns and bounds back to the river, and I bash the catfish's head against a rock and walk back to camp, with a bowl of snails in one hand and a slimy catfish gift in the other. It is by far the weirdest present I've ever received. But it's been a long time since anyone has given me anything and I have to swallow a number of times to get rid of the lump forming in my throat.

That night we have a banquet. A feast of pirahna, snails, nuts, fruit and catfish.

The catfish is disgusting. Pasty flesh laced with bones which tastes like a glue stick dipped in marmite. I manage to force a couple of lumps down then wait until Galaxy is engrossed in eating his share to chuck the rest of my portion into the fire. But apart from the catfish, the food is delicious. I'm definitely getting better at this cooking lark, and with the cunning addition of ground-up mango pulp as a sweetener, my Jungle Tea tastes better than ever.

What a day! And what a way to end it. I'm warm and dry and pleasantly full, and entertained by a laser show of shooting stars and the wide range of noises gushing from Galaxy.

Finally the last nut has been consumed and Galaxy grunts, then nudges my elbow. I raise my arm and he rolls onto his back, snuggles in tight against my side and looks up at me, liquid-brown eyes glinting in the firelight. Too stuffed and comfortable to even bother washing himself, he hiccups, sighs with satisfaction, and soon falls asleep with a dollop of sticky mango juice gluing two whiskers together and his paws clasped together across the vast blimp of his swollen belly. I lick my forefinger and thumb and clean the juice from his whiskers, which quiver like strummed guitar strings then spring back into place. Galaxy gurgles and sighs again and I reach for the piranha-teeth comb I made for him and run it gently through his fur. He scrunches his eyes, folds his paws and sighs, with a look of complete and utter bliss on his face. Then, along with Galaxy's gurgling stomach and the crackling fire, I can hear another noise, a sound like an outboard engine idling in the distance. And I know what the noise is and where it's coming from. It's coming from Galaxy. It's the sound of pure contentment. Galaxy is purring.

THIRTY-THREE

The pebble ploughs into the surface and disappears. I've got the angle wrong, again.

Snatching another one from the pile I bend my knees a little more this time, and skim it as hard as I can, and this one skips eight times before dying halfway to Otter Rock. A new record. I should be pleased, impressed even. But I'm not. I don't care what the pebble does. I just feel sick and deceitful, like when I lie myself into a corner and Mum catches me out.

The past few days with Galaxy have been incredible. The happiest I've been since the crash, perhaps even longer. But now I have to go. I have to get home.

I gaze at Galaxy, licking his nipped nose in the shade of the crooked tree. He obviously lost his first fight with a crab. Part of me wants to use the cut as an excuse to stay and nurse him, but I can tell it's not a serious wound, little more than a scratch really and he'll soon heal. Anyway he learns so fast I doubt he'll be caught out again. He'll be fine. He's healthy and he can fish and fend for himself. He belongs here. I don't. And now he's recovered it's time for me to leave. The longer I postpone my departure then the harder and more painful it's going to be for both of us.

I stamp the remaining stones deep into the sand. I don't feel like wasting any more time on stupid games. I should try and rest now, seeing as I doubt I'll get any sleep tonight. Then I'll fish through the afternoon and this evening I'll cut the laces with my piranha knife and finish the raft. One last massive supper with Galaxy tonight, then while he's asleep I'll fetch the life jacket from the tree, gather my provisions and wait at the water's edge, ready to launch at first light, before Galaxy wakes. He'll be frantic, and scared, I know he will. But it's the only way I can do it. Sometimes you have to be cruel to be kind, Mum says. I think I finally understand what she means. But however much I try to convince myself that I have no choice, and this is the right thing to do, for Galaxy's sake as much as mine, the brutal truth is I'll be abandoning him, betraying his trust and friendship. He'll be alone. Again.

THIRTY-FOUR

My head is throbbing. The sky is dark and at first I'm annoyed with myself for having slept through the afternoon. But as I slowly wake I can see the sky is not night-black, nor even as dark as twilight, and the air is hot and still. Eerily still. I rise and shuffle to the stream, still half-asleep, and as I wipe beads of sweat from my arms I feel a tingling in my fingertips and notice how the hairs on my arms quiver and stay erect, like they do when you rub a balloon fast across your skin and it sticks. I notice how quiet it is. How unnaturally quiet. No screeching monkeys or birds. No hoots or howls. Even the insects are hushed. It's as if every living thing knows something bad is coming and is hunkered down in readiness. I raise my head and see black clouds rolling in from the east, crackling with lightning. A storm's coming. A big one.

I turn and run back to camp. I have to find Galaxy. To make sure he's safe. I spot him almost immediately, fast asleep on top of the log pile, seemingly unconcerned by the storm's approach. Not wanting to alarm him, I gently lift and carry him to the base of the Joshua Tree. At least we'll have some shelter here. Galaxy yawns and stretches his rear legs but doesn't bother to open his eyes. I settle down beneath the tree's dense awning with my back against the trunk and Galaxy's warm body curled in my lap. And in silence I wait for the storm.

Moments later the first clouds arrive, dumping rain and hurling bolts of lightning. My ears pop as rain pelts the trees and the wind howls through the canopy, stripping leaves and snapping branches. A great boom of thunder shakes the sky and I feel its shock wave hurtle down the Joshua Tree's trunk and rattle my spine.

Galaxy's eyes burst open and he stares up at the raging sky. I hold him firmly, with one hand tickling his chin while I stroke his back with the other, and I try to tell him there's nothing to be scared of, but my words are torn away by the wind, and Galaxy wriggles out of my grasp and gallops out into the full force of the storm. I yell at him to come back, terrified he'll bolt into the river and head for his holt. But he doesn't.

He crouches in the open instead, coiled and tense, and when the next flash of lightning comes he barks with glee and bounds to the log pile and tries to reach the top before the thunder cracks. The storm is directly overhead now and the thunder arrives no more than a second or two after the lightning, but Galaxy is so fast he makes it to the top in time and stands on his wooden summit barking at the sky, and snapping at leaves flying past his head. Then he leaps off and crouches a little further away this time, and waits for the next bolt of lightning. It's plain to see he's not afraid. Far from it. He's bursting with excitement. He's fearless. Mad! And his exhilaration is irresistible.

I stand and run out to join him and immediately slip and land face down in the mud. Galaxy whistles and runs to me, butts my forehead and nibbles my hair then runs away. I laugh, and try to chase him around the log pile, but with his clawed and webbed feet it's no contest, and he laps me as I spend more time spread-eagled in the mud than vertical, and even when I do manage to stand the wind threatens to knock me down again. The rain hits hard and fast, BB-gun hard, and each crack of thunder vibrates my bones and tissue. I can't tell whether it's water or blood pouring from my ears.

This is absurd. Insane! What if I get struck by lightning? Or a falling branch whacks me on the head? Or I slip and break a leg. Or I get swept into the river? I should be terrified. I should be cowering in the shelter of the Joshua Tree. But I'm not. I'm dancing in the eye of the storm and I've never felt so invincible. So alive!

I kick my bedding into the air and dance around the fire; I manage two moves before my feet skate from under me and my arse smacks into the mud. Galaxy leaps from the log pile onto my chest, and I shriek with laughter and grab him in a bear hug. We wrestle and roll across the mud, and I hardly notice his fish breath and rasping tongue as he licks my face and yaps. I roll him off my chest and he runs to the other side of the log pile and hides. I don't even bother trying to get to my feet, just scramble after him on all fours.

For the next hour or so while the storm shakes the trees, and pounds the earth and tears the sky, we wrestle and splash and slide, and chase whirling sticks and flying flowers, and each other, and screech with joy until dusk comes and it's too dark to play any more.

I collapse beneath the Joshua Tree. The rain is still falling but the wind has died down and thankfully my seat amongst the tree's roots is above the pooling water. I'm knackered, and soaked to the bone, and bruised all over. But I'm grinning, and glowing inside as well. The storm is fading, and soon it will end, they always do, and when it does I will still be here, and so will Galaxy.

Sometime during the night, when the rainwater snaking down the Joshua Tree and dribbling down my back has made sleep, or even sitting down in comfort, impossible, the last traces of warmth and defiance drain out of me. I so want to sleep, and dream myself into a hot bath, with a soft towel and dry clothes. I want the rain to stop. I want the sun to rise. To feel its warmth. I want this sick feeling to go away. I want this nasty little voice in my head to be quiet. The one that keeps reminding me about what I said I'd do today. The one telling me that when dawn comes I have to go. I have to leave Galaxy. Telling me I have a promise to keep.

THIRTY-FIVE

Sunrise.

At last.

The sky is no longer black. But my mood is. It's still raining. My legs are stiff and sore, my bum hurts and my body is covered in bruises. The fun of last night's rain dance seems a long time ago.

My camp site has been destroyed. My bed's been blown away and all that's left of the fire is a soggy mess buried beneath mounds of leaves and fallen branches. Muddy puddles are everywhere, and the mosquitoes are loving it.

Squelching barefoot through puddles, I take a winding route to the toilet area, head down, trying to spot hidden thorns and splintered branches. I should put my trainers on, or take my time and tread more carefully, but I'm too crabby and in need of the toilet to turn back now.

Rounding the bend I wipe the rain from my eyes and blink and stare at a landscape transformed. The stream has broken its banks and flooded the sandspit. At least two thirds are now under water. Snail Rock is completely submerged. The swollen river is dark brown, flowing fast, and spilling over the lip of the riverbank. A large chunk of the bank opposite has collapsed and only the tip of Otter Rock remains above water, wrapped in weed banners streaming in the current.

I'm stunned, gutted. There's no way I can fish in that torrent, let alone launch a raft, it would be torn apart in seconds. The raft! One glance is all it takes to confirm that the spot where I left my carefully chosen timber is now under at least a metre of water. I take a deep breath and slowly clench and unclench my fists. I need to get my head together, to calm down. The rain will stop and the water will recede. I can collect more wood. I can build another raft and I can catch more fish. As long as I still have my fishing rod...

With a sense of dread knotting my stomach I hurry back to camp, and gaze up at the bare branches of the Joshua Tree. My fishing rod is gone. So is the life jacket. Dropping to my knees I frantically search through the soggy muck, digging under leaves and broken boughs, and I find my trainers first, then my life jacket, buried beneath the refuse from last night's feast, smeared with sticky mango pulp. I quickly check the pockets. Dad's watch is still there. So is the fire glass, and it's still in one piece. Relief washes over me. Now if I can just find the fishing rod I'll be fine.

Squinting through the rain I scan around, trying to determine if any of the sticks nearby have the distinctive bare patch where my palms rubbed the bark away on my fishing rod. But I can't see it anywhere. I grab my trainers and sit on a log and pull one on. I'm staring at the river and trying to estimate how far the wind may have carried my rod as I pull on the second trainer, when I feel an agonising stab in the sole of my foot. Yelping with pain I yank off my trainer, and scrape away a layer of sandy mud to reveal a small puncture wound near the base of my big toe. The hole is too small to bleed but a red blotch has appeared around it and it's starting to burn. I pick up my trainer and shake it, and a small black object falls out, bounces off the log and lands on the ground by my feet. It scurries away. A scorpion! I fling my trainer at it, and miss, then hop back to the swollen stream to bathe my foot. The running water soothes and numbs my toe and I keep my foot submerged until the wound feels no worse than a sand-fly bite.

Splattering a mosquito tapping a raised vein on my forehead, I grind my teeth and take half a dozen deep breaths to try to calm myself. My mood has not improved since waking, if anything it's a thousand times worse. Today began badly and it hasn't got any better. I want to wind the clock back, to start the day again. Or better still, I want to relive yesterday on a loop instead. With head down and eyes scanning the debris, I heel-walk back to camp, on the lookout for thorns and more scorpions. Rustling sounds come from camp. Galaxy's back. Good. I could do with cheering up, and with the river so high and fast I won't be leaving today after all. Perhaps my luck has changed and he's caught me a fat piranha for breakfast. Or more likely he's brought me a slimy catfish instead. I'll find out soon enough.

I raise my head. And see the pig. Stocky and wide, its hairy black back and soiled buttocks are facing me and swaying as it rakes the ground with its front trotters.

A litter of seven or eight brown and white striped piglets are racing around it, playfully nipping at each other and trying to latch onto the saggy teats hanging from the sow's belly. As I stand stunned and motionless, the pig lunges forward and lifts its head with my life jacket snagged on its tusks, then shakes its head. I can see pieces of Dad's watch fly through the air. The life jacket slides off the pig's tusks and she snorts and scoops up a small round object, and in the same instant that I realise what it is, the pig tosses its head back and I hear a distinct crunch followed by slobbering sounds as my fire glass disappears down its throat. Then the pig grunts, lowers its snout, and turns its attention to the rest of Dad's watch.

A red mist descends. I scream and run towards the pig and draw my leg back to kick it as hard as I can. But as I do so I skid and lose my balance and my foot catches one of the piglets instead. The piglet squeals and tumbles into a muddy puddle and the rest scatter, squealing in fear. I fall hard, winding myself, and my thigh slams into the edge of a concealed log which gives me a paralysing dead leg. The sow snorts angrily but to my surprise she doesn't run away. Instead she nudges her piglet out of the puddle and turns to face me, eyes blazing and trotters pawing the earth.

I'm in serious trouble.

The sow is in crazed-mother-protection mode and I'm unarmed. With my dead leg I can't even stand, let alone run. I desperately search around for some sort of weapon. Before I can find anything, the pig charges, emitting a hideous, hostile cry. I manage to curl up in a ball with my arms wrapped around my head just in time, as her tusks graze my forearms, drawing blood.

The piglets are squealing hysterically now and running around in blind panic, fuelling the sow's rage, and she gouges me again and again, lacerating my arms. I try to get up. But I can't. My leg won't take my weight. So I stay curled up in a ball and play dead. But the pig rakes my legs with her trotters and I have a terrible feeling that she's not going to stop until I'm fatally wounded, or dead.

Then I hear a whine, long and shrill, and through a gap between my arms I see a blur of brown. Galaxy leaps onto the pig's back and sinks his teeth into her shoulder. The sow bawls and twists her head, trying to reach him. But Galaxy holds on with his claws hooked in the sow's hide as she runs and spins in circles. Then she rears and bucks, throwing Galaxy off, and he twists in the air, landing on his feet between the pig and me. He spins to face her, back arched and fur bristling, ears pressed flat against his head, teeth bared. A continuous high-pitched wail is pouring from his mouth. Galaxy's less than half the pig's size and a third of her weight yet he's warning her to stay away. To leave me alone. But the pig is too enraged to heed the warning and she charges again.

Galaxy holds his ground. Then at the last moment, just as the pig is upon him, he jumps vertically, like a coiled spring suddenly released. But the pig rears as Galaxy leaps, and he's not quite high enough to clear her thrusting tusks. One slams into his stomach while the other catches him full in the face, entering his mouth and ripping through his cheek. Galaxy's body crumples in mid-air and he slumps to the ground and lies in a heap. Not moving.

The pig glares down at Galaxy, and starts to trample him. She clamps her mouth around his head. Something explodes in my brain. A blinding eruption of rage and hate that ignites every nerve and fibre in my body. I lurch forward, dragging my dead leg, and I punch the pig as hard as I can in the side of her head, over and over, until I'm sure my wrist is broken, and I can punch no more. But I've landed enough blows to stun the pig and make her release Galaxy, and I claw at her face, and jam two fingers into her nostrils and force my thumbs into her eyes. The sow yelps and jerks her head and I bite her neck and try to tear her throat out. But her hide is too thick and my jaws are too weak, and I gag on the mouthful of bristly hair and have to let go. I jump on her instead. Her legs buckle and she topples onto her side, thrashing trotters hammering my kneecaps. Grabbing her ears I push her face down into the puddle, and use all my weight to force her snout beneath the surface. I can feel her heart thumping hard and fast against my chest and it takes all my strength to keep her head beneath the surface, but I'm too consumed with hate to let go. Then the bubbles from her mouth die to a trickle and her heartbeat slows. I just have to hold on for a few moments more and it will be over. And then I hear it; the pitiful cry of pain and loss Galaxy makes when he dreams of his absent mother. I lift my head, and stare at his crumpled form. But Galaxy hasn't moved, and he hasn't made the sound. One of the piglets has.

The piglet is standing at the edge of the puddle, so close to me I can see a white crescent-shaped scar on his pink snout and raindrops clinging to his eyelashes. I growl at him and he runs, but after a few skittering paces he turns and walks back, stamps the water and cries again, the same pleading cry of distress and fear as before. I feel his mother's heart thump hard beneath me, and tiny bubbles stream from her mouth, and with her last pulse of life she tries to break my grip and rise, to defend her young.

I look at the piglet, then Galaxy, and with a howl I slide off the sow and drag her head from the water.

As soon as her snout hits the air the sow shudders and retches, and muddy water and snot stream from her nostrils.

Crouching on all fours over Galaxy's body, I glare at the pig and snarl. My blood is still boiling. If the sow makes one move in our direction I will kill her. No question. No second chance.

All eight piglets crowd around their mother, butting her face and urging her to stand. After a few faltering attempts she does so, and looks blearily in my direction. I can tell by her glazed eyes and drooped head that the fight's been knocked out of her. The piglets are clamouring for attention now and the sow lowers her head, sniffing and licking each mucky face in turn, as if counting them, before turning and trotting away, tail swishing, her piglets swarming around her, squealing impatiently and climbing over each other to reach her swaying teats.

I turn my attention to Galaxy. Lying on his side, he's breathing hard, eyes closed and mouth open. Pig drool covers his face and blood oozes from the hole where the tusk pierced his cheek. Slivers of white bone are visible in the wound and it's clear his cheekbone is broken. The skin appears to be intact on his stomach but I have no way of telling how badly injured his insides may be.

As I dip my trembling hands in the puddle and carefully wash the muck from his face, Galaxy opens one eye and chirps, and weakly paws at the ground, trying to stand. I place my palm firmly on his side, making a shushing sound, and sit beside him, then gently lift him to my chest. In a stuttering voice I start to tell him off for being so stupid as to attack the pig. As I speak he never stops chirruping with affection, his eyes never leave mine, and he stretches his head up towards my face. I lift him a little higher and he nuzzles my neck, and even though he is clearly in great pain he licks my hand, wincing as he does so. My heart feels like it's being ripped in two and I'm close to breaking, but I know I have to keep it together. I have to be strong, for both of us.

Then Galaxy does something he's never done before. He lifts his paw and tenderly strokes my cheek, like I would do to him, as if to reassure me that everything is OK. Then he lowers his front leg and places his paw in my palm and sighs. I stare down at his tiny paw clasped in my hand and his liquid-brown eyes gazing up at me, full not just with pain, but with trust and friendship as well, and the tears come. And I can't stop them. My shoulders shake and sobs rack my body, and I hold Galaxy as tightly as I dare and bury my face in his fur. Galaxy grunts in puzzlement and laps at the salty tears dripping from my chin, and makes his *Give me more!* cry, and his demand is so unexpected that I laugh, and my croaky laughter eases the choking pain lodged in my chest.

Galaxy chirps in response and I gently squeeze his paw, and kiss his muddy forehead. I have no way of knowing how serious his wounds are, and I have no idea how to heal him. All I know is that he risked his life to save mine and now I have to find a way to save his. As long as he lives, I will never leave him.

THIRTY-SIX

The blossom floats for no more than a second or two before the raindrops pummel it under and it sinks to join the countless others I've tossed in the puddle since yesterday. The endless, monotonous rain continues to fall. It's been three days now since the storm, as if a switch has been flicked from 'Dry' to 'Wet' and the monsoon season has begun.

With 99% of the sandspit now under water we're confined to a small patch of mud and puddles around the base of the Joshua Tree, and even this is shrinking by the hour. It's only a matter of time before the river claims this last scrap of solid ground. At the rate the rain is falling that could be hours rather than days away.

There's no escaping the rain. No shelter beneath the leafless trees. No way to get warm or to keep

Galaxy's wound dry, and I don't know if I should anyway. Galaxy is asleep in my lap, tongue lolling, and even with the cold rain saturating his fur, his body is hot to the touch, his breathing fast and uneven. It's clear he has a fever and the bulging lump on his cheek tells me his wound is badly infected too.

My physical condition isn't much better. Most of my body is badly bruised, or scratched, or both. Nasty cuts crisscross my forearms, my wrist is swollen and my kneecaps ache from the pig's kicks. But my foot is the worst. It throbs constantly, the two toes closest to the scorpion's sting are black and twice their normal size, and a purple stain is creeping along my foot towards my ankle.

The only way I can bear to put any weight on the foot is to numb it first by immersing it in cold water for an hour or more, which actually isn't much of a problem since I'm surrounded by cold water and there's nowhere left to walk to and nothing else to do. Lifting my foot from the puddle, I prod the skin, which is waxy and tender to the touch, and the purple hue now covers over half its length. I don't understand it! The scorpion's strike barely broke the skin, and it was over in milliseconds, and in that time it can't have pumped more than the tiniest amount of venom into me. But the poison is spreading fast and without nourishment and medication my body can't fight it.

I have neither. No food. No medicine. Also, no shelter, no fishing rod, no means to light a fire, and no way to build a raft. But even though I can hardly believe how everything could go so wrong so quickly, my mind is surprisingly calm and clear about what I have to do. I have to leave, and I have to take Galaxy with me.

'The process of elimination', Dad calls it. It's simple really. If we stay, we'll die, either by drowning, poison, starvation or animal attack. There's no fruit left on the trees. Galaxy can't catch fish to feed himself, and I have no way of catching or cooking fish either. And with no smoke from a fire to keep them away the mosquitoes are back with a vengeance. My spear and club are gone and I can't protect us if the pig returns. Or worse still, a jaguar finds us. Attempting to walk out through the jungle has never been a realistic option, and with the state my foot's in, it's definitely not possible now. And no one's coming to get us.

So I can't walk and I can't wait. But I can float, and I can swim, and I still have Dad's life jacket.

Caimans hunt at night so we'll only travel during the day and I'll make sure we're out of the river before nightfall. As well as caimans and piranhas to evade, there will be rapids to negotiate, and no doubt a number of other nasty surprises to overcome. It wouldn't take much of a blow to open my wounds and if that happens then my blood will attract piranhas like wasps to jam so I'll have to avoid sharp rocks and other obstacles. But even with my bad leg I reckon that as long as I'm careful and stay focused then the speed of the river might work in our favour. Anyway, I have no choice. I need food and medication fast, and so does Galaxy.

Something brushes across my foot and I look down just in time to see a whirlpool of yellow petals churn and twirl away. The river has claimed the last puddle. I'd underestimated how fast it was rising.

Wriggling my legs out from under Galaxy, I brace myself against the Joshua Tree's trunk and stand on the toes of my one good leg to place my trainers as high up in the tree as I can, next to my jeans, already tied around a branch. The jeans are far too big for me to wear now and too heavy to swim in, and the trainers are of no use to me either. Without laces they'll quickly be pulled from my feet by the current and I can't fit my swollen foot inside the right one anyway. And I want to leave something behind. Something that might be found one day. Something to show I was here. I kiss the Joshua Tree's trunk and mouth 'Thank you' to her. During many long periods of boredom before finding the otters I thought about carving my initials into her bark, or cutting slits to record each day's passing, but for some reason I never did. Now I'm glad I didn't. It wouldn't have been right.

Dirty brown water laps over my feet. Galaxy wakes, looks up at me and chirps. I stroke his head then pull my T-shirt a little further down my body and wish I still had my pants to tuck it into. The T-shirt is cold and musty, with one sleeve hanging off, but it's the only thing I have left to wear and at least it will provide some protection from the abrasiveness of the life jacket.

The water's tugging at my ankles now. I have to hurry. I quickly tie the life jacket's side strings tight and pat the lumpy pocket, checking again that what's left of Dad's watch is secured safely inside.

Finally I close my eyes and take a moment to try to remember the camp site the way it was the night of the banquet. Warm and dry. Mounds of food. A crackling fire. Shadows of flickering flames dancing across my lovely bed and bouncing off the log pile. The sky ablaze with shooting stars, and the sound of Galaxy's purring when I combed his fur.

Galaxy chirps again, more urgently this time, and I open my eyes and look down to see him half submerged in muddy water. It's time.

I sit in the cold water with my back to the river while Galaxy clambers onto my lap. He tries to settle down but before he can I give him a quick hug of reassurance and kiss his forehead, then hold him at arm's length, facing me, hoping he is able to swim unaided and he stays close.

Making the final move is even harder than I thought it would be, and I know that once I do there can be no turning back. But I also know I have to. I have to be strong, and believe I can do this. I glance upstream. The river is free of debris. Eyes locked with Galaxy's, I place my foot against the Joshua Tree's trunk, and push.

THIRTY-SEVEN

Back in his watery element, Galaxy rapidly perks up and for the first hour or two he keeps pace with me, sometimes even leading the way. If he wanders too far into the flooded forest then the *To me!* whistle soon brings him back.

Thankfully I'm doing better than I expected as well. The current is running at a manageable speed and the life jacket handles my light weight with ease. The cold water soothes my foot and I am able to frog kick with both legs and concentrate on avoiding the branches of half-submerged trees and other obstacles, while keeping an eye on Galaxy.

At times it's hard to know where the river ends and the jungle begins, but I make sure we keep to the calm water at the river's edge, out of the racing midstream current.

Besides having to make an occasional detour to avoid trees and rafts of vegetation, the swim is uneventful, and I only catch a glimpse of two caimans, both resting and showing no interest in us at all. I almost welcome the break in the monotony when a flock of many hundreds of parakeets streams overhead, piercing the murky air with their cries and peppering the water with their poo, a dollop of which splatters on my forehead. Surprisingly I don't freak out and hurl abuse at the bird, but grin instead. Gran used to say it was good luck if a bird pooped on you, and the deposit makes a warm, if smelly, change from raindrops.

But then sometime late in the afternoon it's as if Galaxy's fuel tank runs dry and he starts falling further and further behind. I have to turn and fight the current to reach him half a dozen times, tiring myself out and losing precious daylight each time, and when I do reach him he tries to climb onto me to hitch a ride, scratching my arms and neck and half drowning me in the process. So I try swimming on my back, with Galaxy perched on my chest. But it's no good, he keeps sliding off and I can't keep hold of him and see where we're going at the same time.

I'm busy trying to balance Galaxy high on my chest with one hand and stop him digging his claws into my neck with the other, when I feel a bump on the back of my head. I turn to see some sort of fruit or seed pod the size of a coconut bobbing in the water, with a fierce-looking red centipede prowling through the husk. I frantically push the pod away before the centipede can clamber onto me, but then it dawns on me that the pod's insides might be edible, so I splash it until the centipede abandons ship and snakes away towards the nearest tree, all legs paddling. Then I grab the pod and head for shore.

With a numb leg and three other aching limbs, I struggle to climb up the bank, but thankfully Galaxy is able to scramble to the top unaided, and while a welcoming party of parrots screech alarm at our sudden appearance, I quickly take off the life jacket and place the pod on the ground. One blow with a sharp rock is all it takes to split the husk. I eagerly rip it in two, but as I do so a foul smell fills my nostrils and a black slime oozes from the pod. The insides have been liquefied. I fling the pod into the river in disgust. Perhaps I should have grabbed the centipede instead.

As the numbing effect of the cold water wears off, my foot starts to throb and the hunger pangs return. I need to find something to eat, for both of us. But a quick inspection of our landing spot confirms there are no fruit or nuts on any of the trees and the ground is just mud and puddles. And with dusk approaching I don't dare leave Galaxy alone to search for food in the jungle. Starving or not, I won't leave him unprotected.

THIRTY-EIGHT

So cold. So bitterly cold. The night air feels much colder than the river water, and without the heat of a fire to warm me and dry my T-shirt I'm shivering uncontrollably, with goose bumps covering my arms and my teeth chattering. I try walking around, vigorously rubbing my arms and slapping myself to generate some heat, but my foot hurts too much to stand for long, and I know I should save my strength for tomorrow's swim. The only way I can get any respite from the cold is by curling myself around Galaxy, but while his body heat warms my stomach and chest, my back and sides remain icy cold. I can feel Galaxy trembling as well, whether from the cold or fever, or both, I don't know. But the combination of cold and hunger, and fear of what may be lurking in the darkness, locks all my senses on high alert and makes sleep impossible.

Sometime during the night, when I'm wrapped tightly around Galaxy and battling my imagination, I think I sense something big and heavy emerging from the river and entering the jungle no more than a few metres away. I cannot tell if it's real or another figment of my imagination, so I keep as still and silent as I can and hold Galaxy even tighter until my stressed senses slacken just enough for me to accept that the threat has gone.

Eventually the sky pales, birds begin their boisterous dawn chorus and I can distinguish where the ground ends and the river begins, shrouded in mist.

Galaxy is still asleep and I decide not to wake him. I stand, but as soon as I do a sharp pain radiates out from my foot, and I crumple to the ground and grab my ankle. My entire foot is dark purple, almost black, and the bruise-coloured stain is creeping up my leg. Yesterday's swim must have accelerated the poison's advance.

Gritting my teeth, I hobble to the river, slide down the bank, and gulp the brown water. I'm about to immerse my foot when I hear a slithering sound on my right and I turn my head to see a massive snake sliding down the bank and into the river. Its rippling body is at least five metres long, and as thick as my leg, its head bigger than my fist, with a livid red stripe across its eyes. I've seen more than enough documentaries to recognise it immediately – an anaconda, king of the constrictors, and a snake that big would have no problem suffocating and swallowing an otter whole. Or me.

Time to go. I hobble back to Galaxy. He wakes at my touch and chirps for food. But after seeing the anaconda I'm in too much of a hurry to leave to spend any time searching for something to eat.

Somehow or other we make it through the day, swimming as best we can, with Galaxy falling behind more often, and the rest periods becoming longer and more frequent as the day wears on. It's already dusk by the time I find somewhere to exit the river, and then the night passes like the previous one, cold and wet, and thanks to a troop of quarrelling monkeys, sleepless. And still no food.

THIRTY-NINE

A grey light seeps through the canopy. A new day has begun. The third, I think, since leaving the camp site but it could be the fourth, or even the fifth. I can't be sure any more. It doesn't really matter. All that matters is I'm still alive. And so is Galaxy. But the lack of food and sleep is killing me. My stomach cramps are becoming more frequent and more painful. I'm exhausted. I ache all over. The purple stain has reached my knee and I can no longer bend my leg fully, nor feel my toes.

And I'm seriously concerned about Galaxy. He's even skinnier than the day I found him in the holt, and without food I don't know where he's getting the energy to keep going. The lump on his cheek now covers half his face, closing one eye and pulling his gums back to expose his teeth. Most worrying of all, he's much quieter than before, sometimes not making any noise for hours at a time, and I can only assume it's too painful for him to do so. But still he won't quit.

I pick him up. He winces and his tail stiffens, curls upwards and trembles but he doesn't utter a sound as I carry him to the river. I stand waist-high in the water, supporting him with one hand under his chin while the cold water bathes his face and he takes a drink. Then I slowly move my hands away. But as I feared, he sinks almost immediately and struggles to keep his head above water. He's much weaker than yesterday and no matter how hard he tries, it's clear there's no way he can swim unaided. But I already know I can't carry him on my chest. I can't steer with only one arm free, and even with the life jacket's support I can't kick hard enough with my one working leg to keep both our heads above water at the same time. I have to find another way.

I carry Galaxy back to the bank and sit with head in hands, and try to block out the clamorous jungle while I think. There has to be another route. There has to be! I just have to find it. A loud buzzing interrupts my concentration and I lower my hands to find a red dragonfly inspecting my tangled hair. I try to grab it and it spins and darts out across the river to join its mate jigging above a mat of giant lily pads racing by in midstream. As I watch the mat disappear from view my attention is caught by a wisp of grey in the distance. I gasp, hardly daring to believe that what I'm staring at is what I think it is. I wade out a little way from the bank to get a better view and now I'm 100% sure. I've seen the same thing enough times when returning to my camp site. It's a beacon. A signal. It's smoke.

I know what we have to do. We have to ride the midstream current. It's risky. Suicidal even. But smoke means fire and fire means people. I don't know how long I've got left before the spreading poison paralyses the rest of my body. And Galaxy is dying. I have no choice.

I take my life jacket off and wrap it around Galaxy, loosely tying one of the straps across his back. He squirms and tries to bite the string but he's too weak to resist for long, and with lots of stroking and reassuring noises from me, he seems to understand I'm trying to help him and he settles down. I make a loop in the other strap and secure it around my wrist, and before the sensible part of my mind can convince me what a bad idea this is, I push the life jacket ahead of me with Galaxy on board, and swim out towards midstream. Without the buoyancy of the life jacket to counter it, my poisoned leg drags like an anchor in the slow-moving water, but as soon as we enter the central current the sudden increase in forward motion lifts my leg and I barely need to kick with the other one. It's working! Better than I could have hoped, and I can tell by the rate at which the trees race by that we're travelling at least five times faster than before. But the increase in speed comes at a high price. The mid-river water is much rougher than closer to shore and continuously buffets the life jacket and breaks over my head. I'm swallowing too much water, and the effort required to keep Galaxy on board the bucking life jacket, and my head above the waves at the same time, rapidly saps the little strength I have left. I can't keep going like this. I need a break.

With great difficulty I turn side on to the current and try to push Galaxy through the choppy swell towards the dark smudge of trees in the distance, but I've been so focused on simply keeping us afloat that I hadn't noticed how much faster and more powerful the current has become, and I can't break its grip. Now sharp spray stings my face. Squinting through the spray I see a blurry bank of white breakers ahead, barricading the river, and I hear a sound I recognise from the river above camp. But this time it's much louder, and far more alarming. Rapids!

I grab the life jacket with both hands as we're swept into the middle of a seething, boiling mass of angry water, studded with rocks. I careen through it, spinning and bobbing, desperately trying to keep hold of the life jacket and Galaxy. But the current is too strong. It slams me against the rocks and the life jacket is ripped from my grasp. I'm dragged under and I tumble across the riverbed, somersaulting helplessly, slamming into rocks and desperately trying to claw my way to the surface. But my bad leg is like an anchor, weighing me down, and I can't escape the undertow. The thundering current pounds my skull and my lungs feel as though they will burst through my chest. Somehow I find the strength to fight and claw and kick with my good leg, and I haul myself up through the water, towards the light, until I burst through the frothy surface, gasping for air and spewing water.

Through stinging eyes I scan around for Galaxy.

I hear him first, desperately calling for me. Then I see him, clinging to a log at the edge of the rapids, battered by waves and fighting to keep his head above the water. I try to whistle *To me!* but my lips are too numb, and in the same moment that I see Galaxy lose his grip and slide beneath the surface, a blur of orange drifts by – the life jacket, caught in the current and disappearing fast. In a few moments it will be gone.

Galaxy or the life jacket? I can't reach both in time. I take a deep breath, and swim.

Screeching parrots wake me. I blearily look around and see the log is jammed against solid ground. We've reached the edge of the flooded forest. At last. Gently lifting Galaxy from his sleeping place I lay him on solid ground without waking him. He's silent but he's safe, and he's breathing. I so want to go back to sleep too, and dream, and rest my bruised and battered body. But I can't. I don't have the strength left to hang on much longer. I have to find some sort of crutch to support my numb leg and a way to carry Galaxy. I have to reach the smoke.

FORTY

Another fast-flowing stream. Another obstacle. I sink to my knees. My neck and upper back ache from the strain of carrying Galaxy in the T-shirt sling I've made, and I lift it over my head and gently lie him on the ground next to my wooden crutch.

I want to lie down too. To curl around him, and rest. But I can't. Not until nightfall. I have to keep going, like I have for the last two days and nights since leaving the river and striking out in the direction of the smoke. Since then I've walked from dawn to dusk, with only brief pauses to drink at the many streams blocking our way, and to bathe my poisoned foot. The heat has been unbearable, the insects merciless, and my body is badly burnt and covered in bites and bruises. And apart from a handful of nuts, I've still had no food.

But I couldn't risk travelling at night, or heading into the jungle to search for food. The chance of stepping on a snake or a scorpion, or blundering into quicksand, or twisting an ankle in the dark was too high. So I've had to push on during the day, regardless of the heat and humidity, how tired and hungry I am, how much my leg hurts. Knowing our only hope of survival is to get help before the poison paralyses me completely. Or Galaxy's heart stops.

A quick examination of Galaxy confirms what I feared. With no food for five days he's limp and emaciated, and his lump is a lot worse, swollen to the size of a golf ball with a scabby weeping cyst on the taut skin. There's no time to rest. We have to keep going.

Trying to ignore the gathering vultures I reach for my crutch, but my aim is off, and my hand closes around a clump of leaves instead and something squelches through my fingers. Pulling my hand back I gaze at a purple pulp stuck to my palm, then sniff it, and touch it with the tip of my tongue. It tastes intensely sweet, like fudge, or a toffee apple, and the sudden sugar rush ignites something in my brain. Greedily sucking the gooey substance from my hand I peer into the bush and see more purple berries nestled within the leaves, dozens of them. I pluck a handful and shove them into my mouth, and keep cramming until my cheeks are bulging and I can't fit any more in. The energy surge is astonishing, as if my brain has been plugged into an electric socket, and I pick and cram and chew and swallow as fast as I can, only pausing to spit out an occasional leaf or stalk.

Biting down on something hard I dribble it into my palm, assuming it's a pip or stone. It isn't. It's a tooth. My tooth. I don't care. I simply throw it away and keep chewing. Then I remember Galaxy. Shoving another three berries into my mouth I chew and grind until the fruit is a mashed up pulp, then I lift Galaxy's head and try to prod the pulp into his mouth, but I can't, there's an obstruction. The lump on his cheek has a hidden half, bulging within his mouth and almost blocking his throat. Unless I can find a way to remove it, there's no way he can swallow, and without food his body can't fight the infection.

There is only one way I can think of to remove the blockage. I'll have to lance the boil and drain the pus, like Mum would.

After twisting a sharp thorn off the bush, I wrap my T-shirt tight around Galaxy and clamp him between my knees.

'This is going to hurt me a lot more than you,' I lie, trying and failing to sound convincing as I position the thorn above the cyst.

'Now I'm going to count to five.'

'One, two...' and at 'three' I jab the thorn into the cyst, and squeeze my knees a little tighter as Galaxy's head jerks back. He emits a heart-ripping cry, and I feel his muscles knot as he tries to wriggle free. The scab is thicker than I expected and the thorn can't break through but I keep twisting and pressing down hard until the tip pierces the scabby skin and yellow pus spurts out. Galaxy starts to wail and squirm, tearing at the T-shirt, and in a strained voice I tell him it will be only be a few seconds more, and then he'll feel much better, and I tell him what a good boy he is, how brave, as I press my thumbs into the base of the lump to force out more pus. The pain must be excruciating and I hate myself for doing this to him, but I daren't stop, not until I've got rid of all the infection. So I keep talking to him instead, raising my voice to drown his cries, and only when the fluid dribbling out is more blood than pus, and the lump has collapsed into itself, do I stop. I cradle Galaxy in my arms, still swaddled in the T-shirt.

I can feel Galaxy trembling and squirming to break free as I rock him back and forth, telling him over and over how sorry I am, and I promise I'll never hurt him again, until after a while his moaning stops and his muscles relax, and I can risk placing a morsel of chewed-up fruit on the end of my finger and presenting it to him.

He turns his head away and grunts but I keep my finger steady and talk to him in the most persuasive voice I can muster. 'It's lovely, Galaxy. Even nicer than mangoes. I promise. Go on, try a piece. I promise you'll like it. Just try it. Please.'

Galaxy's nostrils twitch and I know he's caught the fruit's scent and is just being stubborn to punish me for hurting him. But he's too hungry to resist for long and when I move my finger a little closer he swivels his head and sniffs the fruit. He touches it with the tip of his tongue, and licks it, and I can tell by his eyes it's having the same electric effect on him as it did on me.

'Good boy. Good boy!' I say, and gently prod some more pulp into his mouth. He starts to chew, awkwardly at first, only using the side of his mouth away from his wound. To begin with, most of the fruit falls out, but I loosen the T-shirt so he can get his forelegs free and he accepts the next berry whole, crams it into his mouth, and chews and swallows as fast as he can, and after the third or fourth mouthful he even emits a shaky *Give me more!* cry. Relief washes over me.

Although I know we should get moving, I spend the next half an hour or so stripping all the berries from the bush, and it's worth it. With the massive sugar boost energising my brain I feel strong enough to stand, tuck a gurgling Galaxy back in his T-shirt harness, and tackle the stream. I can't see the smoke from here but I'm not concerned. I'm confident I know the right direction to head in, and I'm feeling more positive and optimistic than I have in a long time. Not even the sight of the vultures circling overhead can dampen my spirits and I can't stop babbling away to Galaxy, even though I know he can't understand a word I'm saying.

'We'll be home soon,' I tell him. 'And Mum will spoil us both rotten and you'll have more fish than you can eat. And prawns, and lobsters, and things you've never even dreamed of, like ice cream and strawberries and bananas and cakes and chocolate!'

But all too soon the effects of the sugar rush wear off, harsh reality seeps back in and I don't have the energy to talk any more.

Sometime in the afternoon the trees start to give way to shrubs and tall grasses, and even though I can hardly dare to believe it, I think we might be coming to the edge of the jungle. It's not a moment too soon. I've been pushing myself too hard, with no breaks and nothing to drink since the stream earlier this morning.

Drained and dehydrated, my vision is going blurry, and a massive headache has formed in my temple. Leaning against my stick, I breathe deeply and wait for the headache to pass, but with a loud crack the stick splinters and splits in two. My legs crumple and I fall forward. As I do Galaxy's harness swings out in front of me. I try to grab him and twist onto my back to shield him from the fall. But I can't focus and my reactions are far too slow and the last thing I see is Galaxy thud into the earth, entangled in the T-shirt, before my head hits the ground hard, and everything goes black.

FORTY-ONE

I don't know how long I lie there, drifting in and out of consciousness, but I do remember the harsh cries of vultures, and the prickly feet of flies tapping over my lips and into my mouth, and I remember thinking that I have to get up, and get moving. But I don't want to. Even the slightest movement might jar me out of this place of rest and comfort and bring the pain back. So I let the flies be, and try to drift off again.

But then the voice comes. Softly at first, little more than a whisper, then rising in volume and suddenly sneering and scornful. Telling me I should have done what I said I would, and built the raft and left when I had the chance. Telling me I'm finished. Telling me I've failed. Telling me that Galaxy belongs to the jungle and I should have left him in his holt and not interfered. Telling me if I'd kept my camp site clean then the pig would never have found us and wounded Galaxy. Telling me I'm responsible for Galaxy's pain. Telling me I only brought him with me because I'm a coward and I couldn't face the journey alone, and now if I wake I'll have to pay for my cowardice and watch him die in agony, like the tamarin, and know that I'm to blame.

No!

With all my heart I know that's not true, and I won't listen. I refuse to. I squeeze my eyes shut and clamp my hands over my ears instead, even though I know the voice is inside my head.

But the voice is persistent.

'Why don't you leave the otter here,' it says, in a more friendly tone, 'and go on alone? Then when you find help you can come back for him. It's your best chance of survival. For both of you.'

No!

I can't leave Galaxy. I won't. The vultures will move in as soon as I've gone, and even if I did find help there's no way I could retrace my steps and find him again, not before they'd ripped him to pieces. No. I promised I'd never leave him, and I won't.

I open my eyes. It's dark. As dark as twilight. I scratch angrily at my itching insect bites, annoyed with myself for not waking earlier. But as my head clears

I become aware of how hot it is. Too hot for twilight. I remember the same conditions on the day of the storm. Another storm must be on the way. Thank God! The rain will give us a drink, cool Galaxy, and relieve the maddening itching as well.

A vulture cackles to my left, and I turn my head to check how close it is and scare it away, but I can't see it. In fact I can't see any further than a couple of metres in front of my face at most, and nothing to the sides. I tilt my head back and look at the sky. I can see no higher than the tree's lowest branches. The sky isn't dark. My eyes are. I'm going blind.

FORTY-TWO

Hugging Galaxy tight I stroke the back of his neck, lumpy with insect bites. He's burning up with fever, his face is puffy and his swollen tongue is bulging from his mouth. He needs water and food badly, as do I, but I can't walk, or even hobble without my crutch, and even if I could, I can see no further than an arm's length in front of my face, everything beyond that is blurred or black, and I don't have the strength to carry him to a stream, even if I could find one.

But we can't stay here. Without water Galaxy won't last another night. There's no shelter either, and no protection from the massing vultures. I can tell by the rise in volume that their numbers have grown and some have landed and are skulking in the shadows just beyond the limit of my vision. And I have no way of telling what else might be zeroing in on us as well, alerted to our presence by the cackling scavengers.

Galaxy groans, and a green discharge dribbles from his mouth, speckled with blood. I have to do something, and fast! But what? I have no idea what to do.

I bury my face in Galaxy's fur, inhaling his scent and feeling his heartbeat through my cheek. It's faint and faster than it should be but it's still there. Man, he's tough! Galaxy's not dead yet and neither am I. I can find the strength to get us out of here. I have to.

Gritting my teeth I try to stand, but can't. My one good leg won't take my weight, and I only get as far as a bended knee before my lame leg slides out behind me and the foot becomes entangled in dead grasses. It's no good. My body's too worn out. Too crippled to carry me any further.

Howling in fury, I slap my bad leg as hard as I can, again and again. I need something to blame, to punish for my feebleness, and I wrench my foot from the grass and glower at it. It's twice its normal size and completely purple. Bent backwards by the grass, my big toenail is sticking out at right angles, caked in dirt and dried blood and hanging by a thread. I rip it off and as I do so an earwig-like creature emerges from the wrinkled skin where the nail used to be and slinks beneath my foot. I twist my foot to reach it and stop, and stare. The speck of the scorpion's sting has expanded into a stinking sore of black flesh covering half the width of my foot and speckled with white, and when the white bits move I realise it's not bones I can see. It's maggots.

I jab my toenail into the wound and fork one out, and feel nothing. The maggot writhes in my cupped hand, waves pulsing down its bloated body, and a tiny streak of blood-red foam bubbles from its rear end. It's a dirty, disgusting thief, stealing my flesh, and I should pummel it into the earth or throw it to the vultures. But as I stare at it crawling across my palm I suddenly realise it's more than just a greedy parasite, engorged with my flesh. It's protein as well. Energy. Fuel to power my body and buy us a little more time. Maybe enough time to find help. And that's all that matters.

I suck the maggot from my palm and it immediately wriggles over the edge of my tongue and burrows beneath the flap of loose gum left behind when my tooth fell out. I try to hook it out with the tip of my tongue but I can't, it's wedged in too tight, and gnashing my teeth together doesn't work either, the maggot simply scrunches itself deeper into the crater, and I feel a sharp twinge as its probing pointed end touches the exposed nerve.

Sticking my finger in my mouth, I try to dig it out but I'm too clumsy and my jagged fingernail slices right through the maggot's body and hits the tooth's bared nerve end, and an explosion of pain fills my brain. I bite down on my finger, tearing the skin on my knuckle, and scream, loudly and long enough to scare the vultures to flight. My mouth fills with blood but I resist the urge to spit it out, I can't. I can't waste a single drop of blood. Or maggot. I suck the blood from my knuckle instead, and as soon as my hand stops shaking enough for me to hold my toenail steady, I scoop more maggots from my wound and throw them into my mouth, gulping them down alive, and as I do so a weird thought crosses my mind. The thought that I am a cannibal. No. I am not a cannibal. I am something even sicker than a cannibal. I don't even know if there is a name for the thing I have become, a creature which feeds on its own rotting flesh.

And when I've devoured every maggot I can find, I secure Galaxy in a T-shirt sling around my neck and I get on all fours and start moving. Galaxy swings from side to side beneath my chin like a lopsided pendulum, knocking against my elbows and grinding the T-shirt knot deep into the sore skin on the back of my neck. But still I crawl. My bad leg drags behind me, heavy and useless, but still I crawl. My raw thighs chafe together and sharp stones grate the skin from my trailing foot, but still I crawl. I can't walk. But I can crawl. Even maggots crawl. But I am no maggot.

I can see no more than a body length ahead, and no higher than the tallest grasses but it's enough. Enough to set myself a target. That rock. That stick. That clump of dried grass.

Time no longer exists. Or matters. All that matters is forward motion. So I keep moving, placing one torn and bloody hand in front of the other, blocking out the pain and the cackling vultures, until the grasses unexpectedly part and my hand lands on hard-packed earth, and some part of my brain tells me I've reached a trail, a path to take me to where the smoke came from, and rescue. I peer left and right, but can see no more than a few metres in either direction and I have no idea which way to turn.

Left or right? Left or right?

I can't delay, I have to choose and keep moving. My body is on the brink of total collapse and the loud guttural cries behind tell me that at least one vulture is closing in.

As I twist my head from side to side, frantically trying to decide, Galaxy's foot jerks free of the T-shirt and scrapes my chin. Spasms are rocking his body and it's clear by the way his muscles clench and his paws curl that he's in great pain.

'Hang on, Galaxy,' I say, in a pleading, desperate voice. 'Hang on. We're almost there.'

Then in the gaps between the vultures' cries I can hear some sort of commotion in the distance, and in my mind I see troops of monkeys galloping down the track towards us. I remember what they did to the tamarin, and I know we have to get as far away from them as we can, but with the tall grasses distorting the sound and the vultures' cries filling my ears it's impossible to tell which direction the noise is coming from.

Left or right? Left or right. Decide!

Suddenly my instincts scream at me to turn right, and I've learned to trust them, so right it is.

With every punishing lunge my leg gets heavier, the pauses between each movement longer, and the vultures louder and bolder, snapping at my heels. But still I keep crawling.

Then my hand hits something that spins away with a tinny clang, a noise I haven't heard in a long time. Dragging myself another body length forward, I pick up the object and hold it close to my face and stare at it. It's a can. A Coke can. Dented and empty but still beautiful. From another world. My world!

I lift the T-shirt over my head, gently lay Galaxy on the ground, and look down at the thing the can hit – a rock, light grey on one side and black on the other. The rock forms part of a circle in the middle of which is a pile of ash and a half-burnt log. I hesitate. Then place my palm on the ashes. They're warm! So is the rock. Whoever built this fire could still be close by. I raise myself on to one knee and try to shout, but I can't, my mouth's too dry.

A vulture screams close by, and beats its wings, and I can feel the dusty air blowing across my back. Through fogged and watery eyes I peer at the scavengers but all I can see are dark fuzzy shapes crowding around, towering over me. Their cries grow louder and more hostile as they move in for the kill, egging each other on to make the first move. They want to finish us before nightfall, or the monkeys arrive.

One makes a lunge for Galaxy, its vicious hooked beak aiming for his face, and something explodes in my head, and I howl, and throw the Coke can at the scavenger. I will not let these scumbags take Galaxy! As long as I can see, or hear, or punch, or bite, then the vultures won't have him.

Hauling myself to a sitting position, I lift Galaxy into my lap. He's burning up, eyes rolled back, breathing shallow and erratic. It won't be long now.

I lift him to my chest and lower my head, and in a hoarse whisper I tell him how much I love him, how much he means to me, I tell him to hold on, just a little longer. I tell him he's tougher than this.

Dark shapes crowd around us in a squabbling, screeching ring, wings beating and beaks snapping with greed. They're close enough to smell now. They smell of the decomposing catfish, and the pilot's corpse and my rotting foot. I want to scream at them and wave my arms to make them back off but I can't. I can't scream and I won't let go of Galaxy.

A vulture grabs my toe and tries to tear it off and I kick out at it, and keep kicking until it lets go. Then above the screeching scavengers I hear more noises, faint and unclear, but approaching fast. The monkeys, come to join the kill, and in my mind's eye I see the golden tamarin again, torn and terrified, and I can hear its blood-chilling cry and I swear I'll smother Galaxy myself before I let the monkeys have him.

Then, to my amazement, I feel Galaxy's paw touch my cheek, like it did after he'd saved me from the pig, and with his other leg he claws at the T-shirt and tries to wriggle free. Still he clings on. To life, and to me. Still he tries to protect me.

He won't give in, and neither will I. While there's breath left in my body I'll fight for him like he fought for me, and if these ugly bastards want him they'll have to kill me first.

Scrabbling around in the dirt I pick up a rock and bare my teeth and in a weak, rasping voice I snarl at the vultures.

'Come on then! Come on, you cowards!'

Suddenly a cloud of ash billows over us. The vultures lift away, screeching in anger, and I can hear a new sound. I hear shouting. And then the sound of running feet. Then a voice. A man's voice. And I hear what he's shouting. I hear my name.

'Sam. Sam!'

The man suddenly appears by the fire and stops to catch his breath. Then he crouches down in front of me, his face filling my vision. 'Sam?' he says. 'You Sam, yes?'

I never knew a voice could sound so good. It takes me a moment to compose myself before nodding and in a hoarse whisper I reply, 'Yes. I am Sam.'

The man grins. The widest brightest grin I've ever seen, before jumping to his feet and shouting into a radio, speaking unbelievably fast and laughing as he does so. Then he kneels again and offers me a bottle of water, but I won't let go of Galaxy to hold it so he raises it to my lips and tilts it. The water is cold, and sweet and wonderful, and as it pours down my throat I splutter and grab the bottle for Galaxy. I pour it into Galaxy's mouth. The man gives me his shirt, gently draping it over my shoulders to cover my nakedness.

I mouth 'Thank you', hand the empty bottle back, and close my eyes.

Sometime later I hear more people arrive, five or six I think, or it could be more, running down the track, laughing and cheering.

I raise my head as they arrive. Most hold back, and fall silent, as they allow one man to approach me, and as he moves into range he says my name. And I instantly know his voice. I know his voice!

Dad kneels before me, wheezing heavily. His right hand hesitantly reaches out to touch my blistered cheek while he holds his chest with his bandaged left hand, fighting to get his breath back. Then he throws his arms around me and I can feel his stubbled chin on my cheek. I bury my face in his shirt, and feel his heart pounding and I know I'm not dreaming.

'I thought I'd lost you,' Dad whispers, both hands now cradling my face. He's close enough for me to see the tears streaming from his bloodshot eyes. 'I'm so sorry, Sam. Forgive me. I thought I'd lost you.'

I press my face into his chest and hug him even tighter, unable to speak. And he hugs me back.

A few minutes later, I become aware of a lady crouching next to Dad, and there's something about her, something reassuring enough for me to allow her to lift Galaxy from my lap and place him gently on a sheet on the ground.

'Is... is he going to be all right?' I ask.

The lady looks up at me and smiles, a beautiful, warm smile of glossy red lips and pearly white teeth.

'He's going to be fine,' she says, and taps the side of a syringe with a shiny needle on top. 'These antibiotics will sort him out. They're tough, these *ariranha*. And as soon as your dad lets go we can have a look at you too, *aiy!*'

'Thank you,' I say. 'Thank you.' And then, 'Galaxy,' I add.

'Sorry?'

'Galaxy. His name is Galaxy.'

'Good name,' says Dad, wiping his eyes while he reluctantly rises to his feet and backs away so the lady can have a look at my foot. And only when she's washed and bandaged it, and given me five or six injections, and a litre of eye drops, and made me swallow a dozen pills, does she let a hovering Dad near me again.

FORTY-THREE

Galaxy's back in my lap, sleeping peacefully and breathing with a regular, deep rhythm when Dad crouches down in front of me again. I'm struggling to stay awake but then my eyes spring open as I see a blur of orange in Dad's hand. The life jacket!

'Roberto found it,' he says, nodding towards the man who gave me his shirt. 'And after so long we all feared... but then I checked the pockets, and found this, and I just couldn't give up on you.' Dad hands me his watch. 'Thank you, Sam.' He closes his hand around mine. 'Thank you.'

Before I can say anything in reply I hear a crackling noise and see a phone the size of a house brick in Dad's other hand. He lifts it and listens for a second or two before handing it to me, with a huge smile on his face. 'Someone wants to talk to you.'

I don't want to let go of Dad's hand, or the watch, so Dad holds it to my ear.

After a slight delay a voice comes down the line, crackly and faint, but just loud enough to hear, and there's no mistaking who it is.

'Hello. Hello. Is anyone there?'

I squeeze Dad's hand, swallow hard and bite back tears before I'm able to speak.

'Hello, Mum,' I reply.

ACKNOWLEDGEMENTS

Hannah Sheppard, agent extraordinaire, how can I ever repay your faith, encouragement and guidance? ('Get on with the next book!' I hear you cry.) Seriously though, thank you, Hannah, for believing not just in me as a writer but also in the power of a true adventure story and the timeless magic of a child-animal friendship. Thank you too for knowing the perfect editor for *Alone* – Charlie 'Viking' Sheppard, my uber-awesome editor at Andersen Press who can see the arc of a story like some sailors see currents in water, and whose keen mind and slashing sword spares none in her pursuit of pace and slaying of 'clutter'. Without your wisdom and invaluable input *Alone* would not be the book it is today. To Chloe Sackur, the ultimate demon of detail, eagle-eyed, passionately meticulous, and not afraid to call a crocodile a caiman and a plum a papaya! You are the ultimate copy-editor. To Kate Grove and James Fraser for their amazing cover design and to all at Andersen Press for their commitment and professionalism – what a team!

My eternal gratitude to my first-draft reading team – Eve, Ben, Paul, Lesley, Stu and Mark, with particular thanks to my Irritant and Special Adviser Laura, unnaturally gifted in knowing what works and what doesn't, and wise beyond her years.

To Debbie, for putting up with the illogical dreams of a would-be-writer for so many years without once pouring water on those dreams even though the bucket was poised many times.

To my son Joe, for watching so many adventure, survival and natural history documentaries with me, and for reminding me what a thrill it is to be young. And for believing in the power of never giving up.

To my parents, for showing me the world and for imbuing in me a life-long love of reading.

To Bear Grylls, for inspiring the man in every boy and the boy in every man.

To Richard Bach, for writing *Jonathan Livingston Seagull* and Susan Shaughnessy, for *Walking On Alligators*.

And last but most importantly of all, my thanks to you, the reader, for choosing to give this a go. I hope you find the journey as exhilarating and worthwhile as I did.